'TRAPPERS' RENDEZVOUS

Andrew Jackson was President and St. Louis was no longer the town that Peter Irons had loved. Jackson's bank policies were bringing ruin upon the country and the town had grown slovenly. Because Irons was itching to get the stink of town out of his nose, he was willing to go along with the plans of beaver magnate Pete Burley. Burley had received, exclusively, the news that beaver hats were quickly going out of fashion in London, and he needed Irons to reach the trapping region before his rival Jim Hammond and buy up the pelts at last year's prices. It was going to be a hard journey, and when beaver trappers and mountain men meet, it's a rough rendezvous . . .

TRAPPERS' RENDEZVOUS

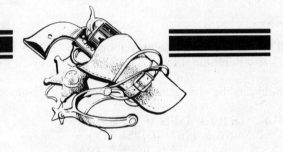

Al Cody

ATLANTIC LARGE PRINT
Chivers Press, Bath, England.
Curley Publishing, Inc.,
South Yarmouth, Mass., USA.

Library of Congress Cataloging-in-Publication Data

Cody, Al, 1899–
    Trappers' rendezvous / Al Cody.
        p.   cm.—(Atlantic large print)
    ISBN 0–7927–0658–7
    1. Large type books.   I. Title.
[PS3519.O712T65   1991]
813′.54—dc20   91–6293
                                                                              CIP

British Library Cataloguing in Publication Data available

This Large Print edition is published by Chivers Press, England, and
Curley Publishing, Inc, U.S.A. 1991

Published by arrangement with Donald MacCampbell, Inc.

U.K. Hardback   ISBN 0 7451 8138 4
U.K. Softback   ISBN 0 7451 8150 3
U.S.A. Softback   ISBN 0 7927 0658 7

Photoset, printed and bound in Great Britain by
REDWOOD PRESS LIMITED, Melksham, Wiltshire

TRAPPERS' RENDEZVOUS

CHAPTER ONE

A man shouldn't be old at thirty. Life should gush as richly in the veins as those giant springs of cold water churning out of the earth and sweeping into the Missouri, not many miles above the Great Falls; it should be red as the haw berries in fall on the eastern reaches of the Rockies. The days came when such truths were easy to perceive, as sensitive in the mind as the musky odor of bear in the quivering nostrils of a fawn. A man lengthened in mind as his step shortened.

On this raw and blustery day, when the wind made whitecaps on the river, carrying in it both a hint of spring and a spit of snow, Peter Irons felt the accumulation of the years upon his shoulders. His gray eyes squinted from under crow-wing brows, peering, dissatisfied, as though hoping to behold the far sweep of prairie or the sheer upthrust of hills which sawed the sky in half. They came back, penned in by the sloppy streets and the sun-faded houses. St. Louis wasn't the town it had been, half a lifetime ago. Half of his lifetime, to be exact, when he'd first come up the river with the high hopes of youth, heading for the Tetons somewhere at world's end.

James Monroe had been president in those

days, shaking a warning finger at a world old and crafty and increasingly rapacious. Florida had been newly acquired from the Spanish; the *Savannah* had made the first crossing of the Atlantic by steam; and life had been good.

But today, old Andy Jackson was somehow in the White House. He'd declared in bygone years that he wasn't a fit man to be president, and now he seemed intent upon proving it. His bank policies were bringing ruin upon the country, and the town was grown slovenly, like a squaw whose man was dead, whose sons had died too young. When first he'd known it, St. Louis had been as bustling and venturesome as a lady, holding her skirts about shapely ankles while preparing to cross a mud puddle.

Today its skirt dragged in the mud, and Peter Irons was not the only one to feel it. There had been a wistful look in the still-youthful eyes of George Rogers Clark when Irons had encountered the Superintendent of Indian Affairs on the street that morning, stopping to pass the time as mountain men did.

There had been a touch of homesickness with the Grand Old Man of the West, and some of the same in himself. Viewing the town on this blustery day, it seemed strange that it could ever have held an appeal. Maybe that clip of the tomahawk alongside the head, two winters back, had addled his brains, as

Shawneen claimed. Right now he should be at the Three Forks, his cayuse gnawing aspen bark and rooting wistfully under snow for a spicing taste of grass. He'd have a fine catch of beaver at their prime peak and be thinking of the rendezvous, of how to get to it with skins intact, including his own.

Instead, he'd wintered in town, misnaming himself a tradesman, working like a squaw, and as little appreciated. Compared to the fortune he'd been sure of, he'd barely made expenses, with the country teetering on the verge of panic and money as tight as a stretched bowstring. A stack of beaver plews, their fur liquid gold in the firelight, would be solid money; but he had no stack.

Shawneen came along the street, choosing his way around the puddles, picking at his teeth with the point of a knife. His overlong thatch of tow-colored hair sprouted from beneath the moth-eaten coonskin like a sack of straw bursting at the seams. The beadwork was popping from his last pair of moccasins, proof that it had been a long time; and his shoulders hunched into the buckskin with a restrained but savage impatience.

Catching sight of Irons, he altered his course, scowling. There was nothing about Shawneen to suggest loyalty, or that he'd left off questing for the lands beyond the sun to follow the whim of the man who once had saved his life and been twice repaid in kind.

3

Had there been the suggestion, Shawneen would have been at pains to erase it.

'You look like a mule with a bellyache,' he greeted his employer disrespectfully, looking up as most men had to. 'I've seen Diggers eatin' grasshoppers that looked happier.'

'At least a Digger doesn't know better,' Irons retorted, and remembered that he'd found three gray hairs among the thick black that morning.

'Now ain't that a fact! All a Digger knows is to live while he's got a chance. He'll stuff one day, knowin' starvin'll come soon enough. But I brung news. Burley wants to see you—quick, if not a mite sooner. Didn't say what about.'

'Pete Burley? But why should I want to see him?' Irons demanded argumentatively. He recalled the day they'd met, hunkered behind a creek bank, knees in the water, while Blackfeet screeched and made their brags of the hair they'd take. He still wore his own, and so did Burley.

'This ol' hoss can't see why *anybody'd* want to see that house-fast child,' Shawneen conceded. 'He's got the smell of town on him strong as an Injun stinks of grease. That ain't the p'int. He wants to see you. An' that's a bigger matter for wonder!'

Irons' long face relaxed to a smile.

'I suppose I've nothing to lose in finding out,' he decided. 'Old Pete's been there and

4

back.'

Which was by way of saying that Peter Burley had drunk of the waters of Manitou; that he had seen the sun rise over Maria's River, and had cooled his feet in streams which ran toward the setting sun. Peter Burley had gone up the Missouri when Sublette pioneered. You mentioned Burley in the same breath with Kit Carson or Jim Bridger.

The main difference between them was that Pete Burley was about as old as Pete Irons felt. In business affairs he was as rich and successful as Irons had imagined himself capable of becoming. Both of them had trapped the Yellowstone and gone into the fur trade for themselves, but Peter Burley had prospered. When you spoke of the Mountain Fur Company you meant Pete Burley. His was the biggest house on the Hill, his name one of the weightiest in St. Louis, where a lot of people had taken to making money and creating a splash—at least up to the time of Old Andy's meddling.

'Hardheaded old mule!' Irons reflected. 'Told me I'd go busted, settin' up for myself. Knows good and well I'm doing it, and thinks now he can get me to head an expedition to Oregon to trap for him! Well, I told him no, and I meant it. Though if I wasn't such a crazy-proud fool I'd jump at the chance!'

It would be the last stretch of clear cold

winter now on the Madison. The midwinter thaw would be past and done, but with signs to indicate that spring was on the way; the slow lengthening of days, the sun more than a faint cold ball poised briefly on the horizon. There would be the restless stirring of the beavers as winter stores ran low and old urges warned that the sun was coming back. Good trapping weather, with the air crisp and frosty like wine in the lungs.

Soon now, almost in a night, things would bust loose. Spring would come with a rush to the mountain country...

The mingled smell of the river and of beaver pelts stored in warehouses wafted along the street. A block-long building, squat and unlovely as the refuse heap of a deserted Indian village, lay almost awash on the river side. Irons strolled half its gloomy length, then pushed open a door, his body filling the frame. He nodded to the spare, nervous man who crouched like a nervous jay on his high stool. At the clerk's gesture he went on to the inner office.

Mountain snows had settled in Peter Burley's hair and refused to melt. By contrast his mustache showed as brown as the second time Irons had encountered him, beside a stinking sulphur spring at the headwaters of the Yellowstone. Despite the white hair, Burley still had the driving force which had made him a leader both among the mountain

6

men and the traders.

'Close the door, Pete,' he greeted Irons. 'Then draw up close. You're the only man in St. Louis I can talk to, and I'm damned glad you're here!'

If the greeting was unorthodox, so was Peter Burley. Irons complied, his interest quickening.

'Wind from the west?' he queried.

'From the east, worse luck. And it carries a smell. London.'

London was a name to conjure with, the chief city of the world, a place of teeming millions. Irons, who could never shake loose the feel of being crowded where a dozen people congregated, had never hankered to see such a human anthill. But London was the beaver capital of the world, even above St. Louis or New York. Because fashion had long decreed that a gentleman must wear a hat of beaver, mountain men had explored half a continent which otherwise would have long lain fallow. London, however unwittingly, held in its grasp the keys of destiny.

'I don't get you,' Irons said.

'Come closer.' Burley's usually strident voice dropped to a whisper. 'I've the biggest news that's happened to this country since Jefferson bought Louisiana from the Little Corporal! At least so far as concerns people west of the river. It's news that's going to hit

7

a lot of people where it hurts—me included, if I don't watch my step! Which I aim to do, with money tight as the grip of a new steel trap and panic spreadin' across the country. Know what? They've stopped usin' beaver in hats!'

'Stopped using beaver—' Irons sampled the words on his tongue, not fully understanding. 'You mean—'

'I've had a hunch for a long while that it was coming,' Burley explained, his voice hoarse. 'As long ago as last summer I heard rumors of a change. In my position it pays to know what's going on, and to know before anybody else. So I've had agents in London for the last year, to find out what's in the wind and to let me know two jumps ahead of the pack!'

He cast a quick glance around the room; moved suspiciously to the window which opened on the river; then resumed his seat. Irons had to bend close to hear his voice.

'Remember Hooker, who came out from Boston and went up the river, three or four summers ago? He never did get over talkin' like he was still on the Common, still he shaped up as considerable of a man! I knew he was wasted here, so I sent him across the Atlantic. He arrived back in town by river boat not an hour ago, bringing me word direct. He was the only man aboard the ship he crossed on who had any suspicion of what

8

had happened. But what's going on in London will shake our world. Styles in Europe have changed. From now on they won't be using beaver. No more fur in hats. Which means that plews will take a sharp drop—down at least half, and maybe a lot worse.'

'That's as bad as smallpox in camp!'

'You ain't palaverin' peace talk! The trappers, Indians and whites alike, are going to find themselves in a devil of a fix. But a man like me—I can be a thousand times worse off. I've already sent my buyers out to the rendezvous with orders to buy at last year's price. Knowing Jim Hammond, I reckon he'll get his fair share of fur—unless he's stopped. If he buys, I'll be no better than a blanket Indian—except that the redskin has a blanket!'

That needed no elaboration. For half a decade there had been ruinous war between the rival fur companies. Now, with panic spreading out of Washington and across the land, this catastrophe topping the rest could ruin the Mountain. If beaver dropped to half its present price when the news broke, as it would before many weeks, such purchases as Hammond would make would be the finishing stroke.

'So far, nobody in St. Louis—and, I venture to think, no one else this side of the Atlantic—knows what is going on,' Burley

9

added. 'I can trust Hooker, and I trust you, so for the present we're safe. There's no other ship from Europe due to touch anywhere in this country for a week. By that time, if the news leaks out, it'll be too late to affect the rendezvous.'

'Though it'll stir up a hornet's nest!'

'Be worse'n a war party droppin' in unexpected on your huntin' grounds! Yeah, there'll be the devil to pay. I want you to start, within the hour, for this summer's rendezvous. You know where it's to be held—on the Green, just across the hills from where the Sweetwater heads. There's not a minute to lose. Jim Hammond will beat you, but you've got to be there before he does much buying. Lucky for me, you're in town. You're the only man who knows that country or stands a chance of makin' it in time.'

He held up a hand to forestall any protest.

'I won't listen to excuses, Pete! I know you're in business for yourself, and that you turned me down when I offered you a job. But this is a different color of hoss. I'll be ruined, 'less you do it for me.' He didn't elaborate or add a plea for sentiment and the sake of friendship. Those were in the equation, but not to be mentioned.

'If you save the Mountain, of course you'll have earned a partnership in it,' he added practically.

Irons was strongly tempted. It would be a

hard journey, and a long one. Spring would change to summer before the distance between could be covered. All that he would enjoy. His temporizing question stemmed from the ingrained habit of caution.

'Why don't you send Hooker the rest of the way? He knows the country.'

'Not like you. Besides, he's been drivin' hard to get here, and he's a sick man. And there's something else!' Once more, Burley lowered his voice. 'Parks, blast his mangy hide, knows something is up, but so far he hasn't been able to find out what. His partner, Higginson, will be at Rendezvous, and if you manage it so that he loads up heavy at the old price, you'll add ten years to my life!'

Sanderson Parks was not a mountain man. It was doubtful if he'd been north of the Platte during the decade that he'd lived in St. Louis. Scion of a New England family, he coupled Yankee shrewdness with an Indian's lack of scruple, with the result that the firm which he managed had come to rival the Mountain.

His methods had brought chaos to the fur lands, and had earned for him the hearty dislike of the older breed of mountain men. But hatred was as a wisp of smoke in his eyes. Rivals had been badly battered during his climb, and now he was gunning for Pete Burley, openly and viciously. He hoped to

11

climb on the wreckage of the Mountain to a position where he would be able arbitrarily to set the price of plews, and hold the trappers at his mercy.

Irons' eyes glinted. He had personal reasons for hating Parks. As for Higginson, Irons was almost certain that the man had set Blackfeet on his trail when last he'd been north.

'That's like meat to a starvin' man,' he conceded. 'I'd admire to do them dirt. But I'm mighty busy, Pete—'

Burley brushed that aside.

'You'll go,' he insisted. 'You can't let me down, and you know it. As partners, I'll look after what business you have. I want you out of town before sundown.'

Irons shook his head regretfully.

'I can't make it that fast. There's a shindig being held at Parks' tepee tonight, and they'll be steppin' high. You know—that big dance he's been braggin' about. My sister Jessica has me hog-tied with a promise to take her, and you know Jess. I've plumb got to do it.'

'Why can't her husband take her?'

'Tom's out of town. She's set her heart on it, and I gave my word.'

'She must of sat on you, to get you to such a splurge. I don't like you going near Parks, even if you do hate him,' Burley grumbled. 'He's got a nose twice as sharp as a wolverine's. But you pull out first thing in the

12

morning. I'll see you again before you start.'

'All right,' Irons yielded. 'For you, I'll do it, Pete. And it ain't for the partnership, though I won't turn up my nose at it.'

Burley grinned.

'Hell, Pete,' he said. 'I know you wouldn't do it for money, but you ain't doin' it half for me. You're like a kid set loose from school, you're that anxious to get the stink of town out of your nose. I'd like nothing better than to go myself, but I've got to stay here and wait to see whether we've any business when snow flies again. Mind you watch your step at Parks'. He'll find out that you've been to see me, and I'd twice as soon trust a rattlesnake!'

CHAPTER TWO

One house in St. Louis rivaled the huge pile of stone which Peter Burley had erected as a monument to his own success. It was a mansion of imported brick, built for Sanderson Parks at a watchful distance. The New Englander had spent money lavishly, and neither New York nor Boston could boast a finer dwelling.

Tonight the house was brilliantly alight with candles and the best in whale-oil lamps. Parks had only contempt for the greasy, evil-smelling lights of tallow from bear or

13

buffalo.

Parks was as far from the typical conception of a Yankee trader as the human frame could manage. Chubby of figure, he had a round race and bland blue eyes. On occasion he could be charming; but at this moment, in the big library, he was wrathfully tight-lipped as he listened to a report brought by one of his many employees.

'Of all the bunglers!' he said savagely, and his teeth, unexpectedly big and white for such a face, clicked through his cigar. Disgustedly he spat out the stub, while the messenger, who overtowered him by half a head, cringed from his fury.

'You've behaved idiotically,' Parks went on. 'I'd shoot a dog so badly trained!'

'We didn't go for to have it happen,' the hapless lackey protested. 'That hoss looked like a dude, but he scrapped like a Pawnee. He jumped quick's a cat after we figured we had him, and come so near to gettin' away that Quint had to floor him with a musket butt. Quint didn't aim to crack his skull. Anyhow, I got a piece o' news for you. Irons had palaver with Burley this afternoon. Burley sent Shawneen to fetch him.'

Parks halted his pacing, considering. Acting on a hunch, he'd given orders, weeks before, that the movements of the two Peters, Irons and Burley, should be closely watched. In view of other developments, today's

14

meeting plainly held significance.

'Well, you've done all the damage you can, so get back on the job,' he growled, and sent the messenger scuttling through a rear door.

Composing his face, he viewed the thronged ballroom, a scene at strange variance with his mood. His glance softened as it rested on the guest of honor for whom he was staging this elaborate ball. Miss Rowena McCoy, of Boston, New York, Washington, Paris, and London, was sufficiently exotic to attract the attention of anyone.

Though tall for a woman, Rowena carried herself with the grace of a fresh-leaved aspen. Her hair, long and rich of sheen, reminded Parks of the prime coat of a silver fox, and her eyes were more green than blue. It appeared as if every man, whatever his age, was clustered about, vying for her favor.

No, not quite everyone. Parks' brows pinched at sight of Peter Irons, but were swiftly restored to smoothness. So Irons was here! But that wasn't surprising. Like a well-oiled clock, Parks' mind grew busy with the possibilities.

Irons stood aloof, as though uncomfortably conscious of his formal attire. The suit belonged to Jessica's husband and fitted her brother well, and to Irons' anguished protest that he felt more at home in buckskins she had turned a white and disdainful shoulder. Parks saw Jessica, the most strikingly

15

beautiful woman present, next to Rowena McCoy. Since her husband was on a trip down to Memphis—Parks' sources of information were excellent—that explained Irons' presence.

Parks did not make the mistake of going to Irons to welcome him. Pete Irons would be instantly suspicious. Parks did better. He contrived, as host, to separate his ravishing guest from her admirers and waft a word to her ears.

'My dear,' he said, 'I'm going to introduce you to a man beside whom these others are pale imitations. I think you'll like him. He's the real thing—a mountain man.' Adroitly he steered her toward Irons.

Irons, following Jessica with his eyes, reflected that she knew how to carry herself at such a ball—better than he, for never would he feel at home in such a place. Five years his junior, Jess was a beauty, and fully aware of the fact. At the moment she was dancing with a young army lieutenant fresh out from the east, a man who looked more at home now than he would likely be on the trail of rebellious 'Pahoes.

Irons caught his breath as Parks came up with a polite word, introducing Rowena. Without understanding how it happened, Irons found himself her partner in the dance.

Here was a woman who outshone Jessica. Or could it be that there was something about

16

her which no sister could quite possess? Irons
had tried unsuccessfully to beg off from
coming, but now thoughts of the trail
vanished. He found himself looking forward
to the remainder of the evening with a
tingling excitement akin to what he had
known when hurrying out in a frost-sharp
dawn to visit his first beaver traps.

Parks watched them as they danced and
was satisfied. Nothing might come of this. On
the other hand, you never knew when a
seemingly trivial incident could be turned to
account. They seemed to like each other.

At midevening, as his fifth dance with
Rowena was drawing to a close, Irons was
jerked back to reality by the sight of Peter
Burley. The older man was not in formal
attire, and something out of the ordinary
would be required to bring him to the house
of the man he hated. The tight, set look on
Burley's face confirmed trouble.

'I've got to have a word with you,' he said,
without apology. 'Now!'

Irons nodded, excused himself to Rowena,
who was promptly surrounded by other
admirers, and followed Burley outside. The
trader stalked to an open space on the big
grounds, away from trees or outbuildings,
where they could talk without danger of being
overheard.

'There's the devil to pay!' he burst out.
'Hooker's dead—murdered!'

'What?' Irons found the transition hard to make. 'How could that be?'

'The fact is that it's happened,' Burley said grimly. 'Don't you see, man? Parks knows something's in the air—something big. Some of his thugs jumped Hooker and tried to make him talk. From the look of things, they started to torture him, and he put up a fight—almost got away. He was a champion wrestler and boxer, you know.'

Half of Irons' mind had lingered with Rowena, the intimate manner she had of smiling, the warmth deep in her eyes, the intoxicating fragrance of her hair. The news jerked him back to reality. The battle for fur between rival companies had of late years degenerated into a ruthless contest in which murder was not uncommon.

'Killed? Do you think he talked?'

'I don't think so,' Burley said grimly. 'It would take a lot to make him, and my guess is that they got in too big a hurry and overreached themselves. But the devil of it is that we can't be sure. Which means that we can't waste any more time. You'll have to start pronto!'

Irons regarded his friend between pity and exasperation. Pete Burley was a formidable figure in the fur industry, but on occasion he lost his head and acted like a grinning Digger. Coming here in such open agitation was an example.

'I checked, and there's a packet startin' upriver in the morning,' Irons said. 'I'll be on it, as far as Wayne City. That'll be quickest, in any case. And I couldn't rush off now without excitin' suspicion.'

'I suppose not,' Burley granted, controlling himself. 'But be sure you're aboard.'

Their conference had not gone unobserved. Parks smiled sourly and congratulated himself on the foresighted measures which he had taken. He had no doubt of the message which Burley had brought, since it was sure to do with the information given him earlier in the evening. That had been inexcusable bungling on the part of his men, killing Hooker instead of getting his secret.

Whatever the news that Burley had brought, Parks was convinced of its importance. Pete Burley didn't hire men to make hurried trips across the Atlantic without cause. Now Irons was involved, and that could mean only one thing. Irons was a mountain man. His job would be to head for the rendezvous with the news, and to carry new instructions. If it was vital to Burley, it was equally so to him.

Irons danced again with Rowena, trying to think of the proper words for leave-taking. A couple of hours before he wouldn't have believed it possible that such a problem could arise. A few dances, a polite word of farewell, and that would be the end.

Now he was fearful that it would be. He was leaving in the morning, and by the time he returned to St. Louis, Rowena would be gone from St. Louis, and from his life. With dismay, he realized that he wanted above all else to see this woman again, to come to know her better.

At the same time he had the uneasy conviction that it was better this way. He'd come from the East originally, and he had a smattering of education. As partner with Burley, he might become fairly well-to-do, although much of that hinged on this summer's work and how well he handled it.

By comparison, Rowena was cultured, poised, charming, at home in the capitals of the world, rich—he groaned inwardly. Better to go as quickly and quietly as possible, and not make a fool of himself. Wanting to linger, he was brief, almost formal.

None of this was wasted on the watchful Parks, who contrived to intercept Rowena before she could be claimed by other admirers.

'A word with you, my dear,' he said. 'And I hope you'll excuse my seeming rudeness. This is most important, not only to me but, I venture to believe, to you as well. Particularly since it involves the man you're to marry.'

'What do you mean?' The glow of the candles seemed to mass in her cheeks. 'Have you had word from Paul?'

'Not directly.' Paul Higginson had been with the trappers since the previous fall, and he would be at the rendezvous, doing the buying for Parks and Higginson. He would never be a proper mountain man, but he knew how to manage an expedition. 'You seem to have made quite a hit with Peter Irons, my dear.'

No woman understood better than Rowena the art of coquetry. In her native Boston, and later in Washington, Paris and London, she had been afforded ample opportunity to bring it to perfection. Part of her charm lay in knowing when to leave it aside. Now she did not pretend to misunderstand.

'Poor boy!' she sighed. 'I like him. He's a real man, as you said. And I'm afraid he rather lost his head over me—or would, if given the opportunity. Probably it's fortunate that we won't be seeing more of each other . . .'

'I'm afraid you're like all your sex, even if a bit more honest than some.' Parks smiled. 'You enjoy making conquests. You appear to have made one so far as he is concerned, and you can count it a real feather in your cap. This is the first time I ever heard of Irons looking a second time at any woman.'

'Really? I thought it was customary for your mountain men to have a woman—an Indian woman—in every camp?'

'So you're interested, eh?' Parks chuckled.

21

'I guess that holds true with a lot of them, but I don't believe Irons ever looked twice at any woman before tonight. But why are you so sure that you won't be seeing more of him?'

'How would I, under the circumstances? Anyway, he told me that he was leaving town the first thing tomorrow morning, for a long journey.'

Parks hid his elation at this confirmation of his hunch.

'Leaving town, eh? Did he say where he was going, by any chance?'

'No, he told me nothing, except that he was sorry at having to go away. You were saying that this concerned me and Paul?'

'It does, unless I'm greatly mistaken,' Parks agreed. 'Did it ever occur to you that Irons might be heading for the same destination as yourself?'

Rowena caught her breath.

'For the rendezvous on the Green? No, I hadn't thought of the possibility. But why?'

Parks did not answer directly.

'I wonder just how much you care for Paul, my dear—how much you'd be willing to do for him, or on his account?'

'I'm going out there to marry him, as you know,' Rowena answered quietly. 'That should answer you. A woman should be willing to do anything to help her man.'

Parks was one of the few who had any inkling of the secret. The matter had been

22

discussed the better part of a year before, when Rowena had agreed to marry Paul Higginson, following a whirlwind courtship.

She had been about to sail for Europe, while Higginson was to leave Washington for St. Louis, thence north with the fur brigade. He had suggested lightly that, on her return, Rowena might journey to the rendezvous and marry him there. She had agreed as carelessly, as they had parted to go their separate ways.

Now, in all seriousness, she was here in St. Louis, proposing to make the trip as promised. Parks had done his best to dissuade her, using every argument at his command save the most potent one, which weighed heavily on his mind. He couldn't warn her of what she might find when she got there, or say that Higginson was likely to be less than pleased. He had dwelt on the dangers and hardships incident to such a journey, but every point short of the truth had failed to move her.

The original idea had been one of the frequent hair-brained notions of his impetuous partner, a piece of folly as soon forgotten as made. He was certain that Paul had never taken the idea seriously or expected her to.

But since she was determined to go, this journey might be turned to account.

'That's what I expected you to say.' Parks

nodded, pleased. 'But not every woman would say it, much less go to any necessary lengths to help her man. And since you're no ordinary woman, I'm going to take you into my confidence. What you do will determine whether Paul and I continue to prosper, or whether the end of summer finds us bankrupt.'

A startled light momentarily replaced the softness of her eyes. That was blunt talk, man-to-man talk. Ordinarily it was never wasted on a woman, and there was an implied compliment that he would discuss serious matters with her on the same footing as if she were a man.

'Bankrupt?' she repeated.

'To put it mildly. Conditions are unsettled in this country, with a lot of people on the verge of panic. But I don't need to tell you that. You're newly come from Washington.'

'I know,' Rowena agreed. She had been back from Europe half a year, and Parks had learned that she could not tell him the latest business news from Europe, but certainly she knew what was going on in the capital. 'People are fearful of the President's bank policy.'

'What do you think of it?'

'I don't know,' Rowena confessed. 'His enemies hate Mr. Jackson fervently, but his friends admire him as sincerely. He may be mistaken, but I'm sure that he is completely honest.'

'I'm inclined to agree with you, and to go along with him as concerns the bank,' Parks said gravely. 'In the long run, I think his policy is a sound one and will help the country. But on a short-term basis—that's a different matter. The mere mention of it has pretty well destroyed confidence, and it's going to hurt more before things improve. That makes for a precarious situation. On top of that, something is happening in Europe—something which has to do with the fur trade.' He probed again. 'You've been in London. Have you any notion what it might be?'

'I?' Rowena arched her brows. 'Now you *do* flatter me. I'm afraid not. I was scarcely concerned with the European angle of the fur industry.'

'I suppose not,' he agreed gloomily. 'And whatever is happening, it appears to have come to a head since you were there. I wish I knew what is going on, for the answer to that will tell whether Paul and I make money or fail this year. Peter Burley is my chief rival—he's the man who came and dragged Irons from your arms so unceremoniously! He's shrewd, and he's had agents in London to watch the situation. I wish I'd had the forethought to do the same.'

Parks had Rowena's complete attention.

'One of Burley's agents arrived in St. Louis

today. He brought a message which has excited the old man as I've never seen him before, so I know it's important. It is so vital that Burley has persuaded Pete Irons to leave his business and head for the rendezvous in the morning—as he partly told you.'

Rowena considered, her mind dwelling on the possibilities, not without a tinge of pleasure.

'You think that this news from Europe is really important?'

'So much so, my dear, that I'm convinced we must learn what it is before the rendezvous is under way. Otherwise, I'm afraid you'll have to wed a pauper, or else postpone it for years,' he added bluntly. 'That's why I'm asking for your help.'

'But what is it that you wish me to do?'

Parks had worked for an elaborate build-up. Now he made his gamble.

'Irons will be heading for the rendezvous, the same as you. You should be able to work it so that you can go along with him; his experience and protection on the trail will be worth a lot. But your real job will be to get that secret from him—one way or another. He's already lost his head over you, so it shouldn't be too difficult. Get the news—and give it to Paul!'

Rowena eyed him doubtfully.

'Aren't you a bit carried away?' she asked. 'It seems to me you're asking a good deal—and wanting me to act unfairly. I like Peter Irons.'

'And he likes you!' Parks shot back. 'That's the fortunate aspect.' He leaned forward impressively. 'My dear girl, it's really very simple. Do you love the man you're going to marry more than you like Peter Irons? It boils down to that. You alone have the opportunity, and—as a beautiful woman—the power to save Paul from ruin. I'll admit that I have a selfish interest; but as Paul's partner, I'm keeping watch at this end of the trail and doing what I can.' His voice took on a regretful tinge.

'I wouldn't ask it of you if I could think of anyone else who could do the job. As it is, it seems extremely fortunate that you are making the trip, though you know that I have been against it. But I'm not exaggerating when I say that success or ruin for Paul hinges on this. I'm not asking you to do anything to hurt Irons or Burley, merely to save us. The decision, of course, is up to you.'

Rowena sat silent, eyeing him intently, then she rose to pace to the window and stare unseeingly out at the dark. The sound of fiddles from the big ballroom, the gaiety beyond the door, was forgotten. Parks did not try to hurry her.

'How would I go about it?' she asked.

'You and your Aunt Lexie have

reservations aboard the *Carrolton* as far as Wayne City. Your plan was to take horses from there, hiring a competent guide and escort. Since Irons will be leaving on short notice, my guess is that he'll be aboard the packet and will follow the same route.

'You can't tell him that you're going to the rendezvous to marry Paul Higginson, of course. But if you can find some plausible excuse for making such an unusual journey, then throw yourself on his good nature and have him make the arrangements so that you and Lexie can go along—'

Rowena reached across to the desk and picked up a quill. She stroked the feathered end absently back and forth across her full lips.

'That won't be difficult,' she conceded. 'As it happens, I have a secondary reason for making the trip—and I can give a truthful answer, without telling all the truth.'

CHAPTER THREE

A day earlier, Irons would have been excited at the thought of what lay ahead, and he could read high expectancy in the seemingly dour face of Shawneen. Only personal loyalty had kept Shawneen in what he referred to as a 'stinkin' buffaler waller' during the past year.

He had grunted noncommittally at the news, but he was elated at the thought of returning to the mountains, of reaching Green River for the rendezvous. It was like a reprieve suddenly given a man waiting out the last hour to the gallows.

Irons had felt the same way. He had stuck doggedly to his business, resisting all blandishments from Burley, but he hadn't been happy. As a businessman he was a better trapper, and now he could admit it with a light heart and joy in returning to the old free life. But a few hours had made a change. This was grim business upon which he was embarking. A look at the murdered Hooker had removed any doubt. His captors had taken him to a remote cabin near the edge of town, and someone had tried the effect of a hot iron, before Hooker went berserk.

That he, in turn, could expect trouble, since it would be certain that he carried the same secret, was a foregone conclusion. That didn't worry him. It was his heart, not his head, that dragged back like a balky mule on a rope.

Only his given word had taken him so abruptly from Rowena McCoy. He'd never paid much attention to women, or to any particular woman, before. The notion that a man could fall violently, head over heels, in love in the space of a few heartbeats had seemed wildly fanciful. But it had happened to him.

By the time he returned, Rowena would be long gone. This was farewell, and whatever Shawneen felt, Irons had the sensation of walking that last journey to the gallows as he stepped aboard the *Carrolton*.

Like the *Yellowstone*, which had recently pioneered a successful trip up the Missouri as far as Fort Union, the *Carrolton* was a packet built strictly for utility, and by no stretch of the imagination could it compare with the floating palaces soon to follow in the river trade. Those were for the Mississippi, not for the still untamed and largely unknown Missouri. The *Carrolton* was a hundred and ten feet long, and its chief virtue lay in the fact that it was of so light a draft that its captain claimed it could run on a heavy dew. Once it got far upstream, it might have to.

Still, it represented luxury compared to Irons' first trip up, fifteen years before. Then, along with dozens of others, he'd plodded along the riverbank, shoulder to a tow rope, dragging the keelboat which contained a season's supplies and barter goods for the Indians. It was to be used in transporting the winter's catch of fur downstream the next summer. Memories of the unadulterated agony of the toiling weeks were still as plain in his mind as the old scars of that galling rope on arms and shoulders.

They'd ride the *Carrolton* to Wayne City,

for the river would take them almost directly west that far. At the sprawling town of Independence, back from the bluffs, they would secure horses and head overland. Irons was no stranger to that route. They'd swing northwest to the Platte, where it began its curve to the north, and follow it to its confluence with the Sweetwater. In turn, that would lead them to the mountains somewhat north of South Pass—and across those rolling hills lay the Green and Rendezvous.

It had a simple sound, but the doing would entail weeks of hard riding, traversing wild country in all sorts of weather. Though starting in spring, it would be summer when they reached the Green. But after a year in the city, even the hardships would seem in the nature of a picnic—if it wasn't for leaving Rowena behind.

Perhaps it would have been better if he'd started as Burley wished, and so missed meeting her. In the next breath, he knew by how narrow a margin he had come by those few hours with her, and that he'd treasure them always.

The Missouri swirled, sullen and muddy, lifting the packet impatiently. Roustabouts were about to pull in the gangplank when there was a sudden commotion. Irons stared unbelievingly, then ran forward. Rowena McCoy alighted breathlessly from a carriage and hurried to get aboard, accompanied by a woman not many years her senior.

Rowena's face lit up with a welcoming smile.

'Mr. Irons!' she exclaimed, and now the coquetry was not forgotten. 'Don't tell me that you're going on this boat, too! Oh, this is delightful!'

She did not say that it was a surprise, but Irons was in no condition to notice her wording. He was inclined to agree with her. Rowena was flushed and breathless as the packet cast off.

'This is wonderful, your being on board,' she declared. 'You didn't tell me you were going upriver.'

'Nor did you tell me,' Irons reminded her. 'I had supposed that you'd be returning East. Unfortunately, I'm not going far by boat. Just to Wayne City.'

'Why, that's where I'll be leaving the boat, too,' Rowena said artlessly. 'Then Aunt Lexie and I are heading for the trappers' rendezvous at Green River.'

Irons gasped, for once taken completely by surprise.

'Green River?' he echoed. 'Rendezvous? Why—you don't really mean that!'

'Oh, but I do,' she assured him, and he noted that, despite the dimple in her cheek, her chin had a determined set. 'I know what you're thinking—that such a journey is unheard-of for a white woman, though our red-skinned sisters seem to accompany their men across the plains without thinking much about it. But that's one of the main reasons why Lexie and I are going—because it's new and perhaps rather startling.'

By now, Irons had control of his wits. 'I'd hardly class you with such "red sisters,"' he said dryly. 'But I'm mighty curious.'

'It's this way,' Rowena explained. 'When I was in Europe last year I wrote several pieces for some of the London papers—articles on pioneer life on the frontier. Don't look so surprised,' she went on. 'I write for money, because I'm a working woman and no heiress, as some people think. Also I knew what I was talking about. It's true that I was born and raised in Boston, but I spent two summers on the frontier, along with Aunt Lexie. We know how to ride a horse and look after ourselves. Anyway, those same papers wanted me to make the journey to the rendezvous and write a series of articles about the experience, and so—well, here we are.'

For the moment, Irons was speechless.

'I'm afraid that I'm unorthodox in my behavior,' Rowena went on. 'I don't do what is expected of women. I not only scribble but I do all sorts of things that cause other women to raise their eyebrows.'

'I think that's wonderful!' Irons declared. He was dubious about women making such a journey, but it had suddenly come home to

33

him that they'd be going along the same route. It was a dizzying prospect.

'Do you think so? It does me good to have your approval. Some men are helpful, but mostly they're only shocked.'

Rowena spoke rapidly, stifling a feeling which would not quite be downed that this was a shabby trick she was playing. Only the conviction, impressed upon her by Parks, that she was working to help the man she was going to marry steeled her to the part. A woman must be loyal to her man, else she wasn't worthy of him.

Irons rubbed at his chin, ruefully feeling the new stubble since the night before.

'It *is* wonderful,' he repeated. 'But have you thought this all out? I don't mind telling you that I'm heading for the rendezvous, too. If you really want to go along, Shawneen and I will do what we can to help, and glad of the chance. But it's going to be a race against time to make it. We're both a bit late in getting started. It will be a hard grind, for everybody.'

'And for women in particular? But it is generous of you to offer, and if you will allow us to accompany you, I assure you we'll be most grateful. I promise that we won't hold you back. Of course, if you feel that we would be a hindrance, we won't impose on your generosity.'

Irons was torn between impulses. Thought

of having her along, all the way to Green River, and of course back again, under his protection, conjured up a vision beside which the expectations of Shawneen were tepid. Her remark that she was no heiress had set his mind leaping wildly. Looking at her slender, graceful sureness, he found himself believing that she could do it, that she would not be a hindrance.

On the other hand, he knew the hardships and perils. Rendezvous, by its very nature, was a wildly boisterous celebration. Hundreds of trappers and Indians, the latter no more wild than the men on holiday, would congregate there. For two women to take that trip—

'If you're determined to go, I'll do all I can to help,' he reaffirmed. 'For my part, I'll be glad to have you along. Just the same, I must say that it's a risky business.'

'I suppose it is,' Rowena agreed. 'But you're a dear, and I'm going. This is Aunt Lexie,' she added, as her aunt came up. 'She's going along to look after me, which I call downright generous, since there's no one to look after her.'

Lexie smiled at Irons, revealing good teeth in a generous mouth. Her hat was small, perched with a hint of daring on her soft brown hair. She held out her hand, man-fashion.

'Rowena was much impressed by her first

35

sight of a real mountain man,' she said. 'Now that I see you, I can't blame her.'

'Oh now, Lexie, I've met mountain men before,' Rowena protested. 'Not that it detracts in any way—' She turned rosy with confusion and changed the subject.

Irons liked Lexie at once. But Shawneen, as he had expected, was scandalized at the prospect of having two women along on the journey.

'You gone an' tooken leave o' what little sense you ever had?' he demanded. 'Ain't we got troubles enough without havin' a passel o' wimmin traipsin' along? Looks like you stayed in that town till it addled your brain. Who is this Lexie, anyhow?'

'She is Miss Rowena's aunt. I've just been telling you.'

''Times a big wind can blow without raisin' no dust. Is she married?'

'She was. Five years ago, Rowena told me. Married and tragically widowed the same week.'

'A widder! Widders are worse'n horse flies. All wimmin are designin', but widders are worse.'

'Don't you like women?' Irons asked guilelessly. 'I figured you'd be that tickled—'

'Tickled? Me? Like 'em!' Shawneen snorted. 'Wimmin are worse'n a hungry belly. I've had me three wimmin—Cree, Crow, an' Flathead. The Cree, she wan't bad,

36

taken by an' large, only she up an' died. I traded the Flathead for a runnin' hoss, and figgered I was lucky. Only trouble was, this ol' mule didn't know 'nough to leave good alone. Went an' affiliated up with that leetle Crow squaw. Purtiest o' the lot.'

For a moment his eyes held a reminiscent gleam, and he sighed so gustily that the fringes of his mustache flapped.

'Purty ain't only skin deep, they say, an' I reckon that feller had had him a Crow when he made said observation. Yeah, she was the purtiest o' the lot, an' the orneriest. Cost me two hosses, a dozen beaver plews, a jug o' whiskey an' a twist o' chawin' tobaccy to get the chief, her pap, to take her back. He knowed her, too. But it was cheap at the price, though I set a heap o' store by that twist o' 'baccy.'

The *Carrolton* was crowded with a motley aggregation. Mountain men rubbed elbows with Indians; teamsters from Santa Fe jostled the rivermen. The four corners of the earth were represented, all different, yet curiously alike in that the land beyond the Missouri had set its stamp upon them. It was a familiar sight to Irons, but exciting to Rowena. Time passed quickly as the river boat churned westward, until, as they neared Wayne City, a message was handed to her.

The letter was addressed in the handwriting of Sanderson Parks—a

37

meticulous Spencerian. She turned it, unopened, in her fingers, while the bearer waited.

'Where did this come from?' she demanded.

His answer was forthright. 'Mr. Parks told me to give it to you 'fore we got to Wayne City,' he explained. 'Mebby you'd better read it.'

Since Parks had driven them in his own carriage almost to the dock, it seemed strange that he had not given his own message. Rowena tore it open, and angry color flamed in her cheeks.

My dear Rowena, Parks wrote. *By the time you read this, I trust that your mission may have prospered. If, as I expect will be the case, you already have secured the necessary information, there will then be no need to risk the hazards of a further journey, which I still feel is unwise. You may trust the bearer of this note. Give the news to him, and he will know how to act on it.*

Her cheeks burned as she considered the impertinence. It was plain that Parks did not trust her to go through with the undertaking all the way. If he had been forthright at St. Louis, it would have been different. Actually he had appeared to acquiesce in her plans, only to gain her agreement. Crumpling the note, she tossed it overboard.

'What's your name?' she demanded, eyeing the ponderous messenger with disfavor.

38

Under her glance, he belatedly removed a shapeless cap and twisted it in big hands.

'Quint, ma'am. I—'

'Then, Mr. Quint, you may return and tell Mr. Parks that I will handle this matter as agreed upon in the first place—which means in my own time and fashion.'

Turning her back, she walked away, still furious. Part of her anger, she realized, came from her implication in an affair which was growing more distasteful by the hour. She agreed with Parks that she owed it to the man whom she was going to marry to help him in every way possible. But did he think her announced intention of traveling to the Green River was just a whim, to be discarded at the near approach of hardship? If so, he'd discover his mistake.

More than half the complement of the packet went ashore at Wayne City. Irons secured lodgings for the ladies at the shack-town of Independence, finding a room a cut above the run and with a landlady who guaranteed respectability. The house was sod, and a homelike touch had been sought by adding long strips of flowered calico over walls and ceiling. These billowed in the faint breeze, producing a bizarre effect.

Irons set about the task of getting good horses for the trip. Though far from reconciled to the prospect, Shawneen accepted the situation with such philosophy as he could.

'I've been charged by grizzly b'ars, chased by Injuns, froze in winter an' roasted in summer. Once I was buried by a snowslide; another time I was chawed by a painter. So mebby this won't be too much worse.' He sighed. 'Though I did think I'd seen things as bad as they could git.'

Irons debated whether to take extra men along, but, after securing Rowena's views, decided against it. The four of them could travel faster alone, and the added protection of numbers in case of Indian trouble would be more than offset by the unwieldiness of a larger party. A few could keep out of sight where several would leave a trail like a caravan.

Experience made its own luck, and he found eight wiry horses that had plainly been Indian ponies. They were shaggy and as unlovely of disposition as of looks, but they could be ridden in relays and endure the journey as well as those who rode them. Descendants of Spanish-imported ancestors, the wild toughness of the land was a heritage in their blood. They were the breed which, trotting all day, could still muster a reserve of speed and endurance if jumped by hostiles.

Giving them into the charge of Shawneen, Irons shifted to a more difficult quest—that of locating a serviceable but lightweight tent which could be pitched at night for the use of the women. There were plenty of tents, but most of them were too big and cumbersome.

Questions led to a slowly warming trail. It took him through the streets and toward the outskirts of town as dusk came down, but at a final shack he was rewarded. The man who came to the door listened in dour silence, then invited him to step in.

'Yeah, I reckon we got what you want,' he agreed. 'Bought one back in Indianny, three years ago. Got it kickin' around somewhere, I guess.'

Only such a suggestion of good news held Irons. He'd slept in overcrowded tepees and companioned with mountain men, and his nose was schooled to smells at wide variance with the clean air of the open plains; but this hovel would have offended a skunk. Scant light filtered through a scraped and rotting deer-skin tacked in place of a window, and as he turned, his host hit him behind the ear with a rocky fist.

Staggered, Irons clutched at a table edge and lifted his boot. He planted it in mid-paunch as his attacker advanced, throwing him against the door with a jar which threatened to collapse the house. But before Irons could follow up his advantage a club smashed out of the shadows behind and darkness came in lashing agony. His knees buckled, letting him collapse at the feet of the other man, who promptly drove a boot toe into his ribs by way of reprisal.

Retching, gasping for breath, Irons was dimly aware of at least four men crowding above.

'Damn your mule's hide, Zeb, what'd you want to hit him so hard for? If'n you've cracked his skull, we won't get a danged copper for him.'

'I was only stoppin' him from killin' you,' Zeb retorted. 'Anyway, he ain't kilt. Got a head like a rock, an' that pelt o' hair an' cap besides. He'll be more ready to talk for a bit o' workin' over.'

'Throw a bucket of water in his face,' suggested a third. 'That'll stir him up.'

Someone obeyed, sending it sloshing over his head and chest. Irons moaned, but the pain in his skull was too great, the darkness receding only to advance. He lay limp, and presently whiskey was forced between his teeth, a blinding bite of the strongest liquor he'd ever tasted. He choked and gasped and was able to sit up uncertainly, back to the wall, then to pry his eyes open.

'Told you he'd come around,' was the comment. 'How you feelin', old hoss?'

'I've felt better,' Irons confessed, his thick tongue slurring the words. He'd been a fool. Hooker had been murdered back in St. Louis for information which he possessed. He should have been an old-enough hand not to walk into a trap. But the reflection brought

42

no comfort.

'Well, you can have your choice of feelin' better or a sight worse,' the club wielder informed him. 'I reckon you know what we want. You got news from London, that you're takin' to Rendezvous. Only this is as far as you go. You can tell us easy, or we'll get it out of you the hard way. Take your choice. It don't make much diff'rence.'

'Go to hell,' Irons said sourly.

'You'll wish *you* could, 'less you start talking. It'll be a pleasanter place than here if we have to work on you. Tie him good, boys. He's a stubborn critter.'

The others obeyed. This was a bad part of a dubious town where anything was customary rather than the exception. Moreover, the shack was so remote that no one would be likely to hear even if he raised a ruckus, or to investigate. Sweat broke coldly on Irons' face.

A smoldering blaze in the fireplace flared higher as wood was piled on and an iron poker thrust into the flames. This was the same pattern that had been tried with Hooker back at St. Louis, and some of these men were probably of the same crew. They had undoubtedly come upriver on the same packet with Irons.

There were no chairs, but as the light grew brighter, he saw the tent he'd been seeking, folded and stowed on a shelf. At least there had been a nubbin of truth in what he'd been

43

told.

Zeb worried a bite from a twist of black leaf, pulling and tugging like a buzzard above carrion. He spat at the leaping blaze.

'Be easier to wag your tongue than chew on it,' he warned. 'What good'll it do to play mule? *You* won't get to Green River nohow—special' if we have to work you over.'

He waited; then, as Irons made no reply, instructed the others to pull off his boots.

'Me, I'm artistic,' he declared, and lifting the poker, squinted at the red-hot tip. 'Also, there ain't nothin' purtier'n a man's skin for drawin' pictures on—tepee, mebby, an' a crick alongside, an' trees. Or you can do a nice job on a man's foot. On'y trouble is, he cain't walk again for half a year, an' sometimes they never get so's they can more'n hobble. I 'member one ol' buffaler like that. He was stubborn as all get-out. I fin'ly had to start on his stummick, after puttin' out one eye, and then his tongue got to clackin'. Blubbered like a baby, he was that eager.'

Irons steeled himself for the ordeal. It looked hopeless, but the effect of the blow on his head was wearing off, and even with hands and legs tied, he'd make out to give them their money's worth. Foreseeing this, Zeb spat again and issued his orders.

'Crow, you straddle his middle. Quint, you roost on his chest. An' you, Mule, set on his

44

legs. I don't like a man to wiggle too much when I'm workin'. Spoils my doing a good job.'

Now the tip of the poker was white-hot, red extending back for half a foot. As the others prepared for their role, Irons drew his legs back and lashed out, catching Zeb in the groin and hurling him across the room and into the fire. His howl would have done credit to a Comanche as he clawed free of the flames.

Twisting, Irons rolled into Mule, bringing him down half on top of himself, but Mule reared back with a bellow to rival Zeb's. Irons saw that he'd laid a thigh across the dropped poker, which was eating a black mark along the floor puncheons.

Irons brought his hands about, careless of a burn, felt the eating force of heat along his wrist, and then the rope was severed and his arms came free. He rose to his knees and wrapped his arms about Quint and pulled him into the melee. It was a kicking, striking, clawing ruckus; the most fun he'd had since holing up at St. Louis, though he wished his legs were free.

In the midst of it a woman screamed, then Shawneen's voice boomed from the doorway.

'Heave back 'fore I let go this charge o' buckshot! An' I got a mighty itchy trigger finger!'

CHAPTER FOUR

Shawneen leaned against the stock of a muzzle-loading shotgun whose blast was worse than its thunder, flanked by Rowena with a long rifle and Lexie with a pistol in either hand. Before that formidable array the others goggled and surrendered. Irons, his legs freed, got unsteadily to his feet, and Rowena eyed him between pity and horror.

He'd given rather more than he received, but during the process the quartet had gotten in some pretty good licks. His shirt was ripped to shreds, one eye was closed, his face battered. The hot poker had seared his left arm in a blighting encounter; a knife had gouged his thigh. There were other sundry bruises not visible to the casual glance.

'Merciful heavens!' Lexie exclaimed. 'What a country! I think I'm going to faint!'

Shawneen gave her a look of disgust, but Rowena's voice was crisp and cool.

'You know you never do that, Aunt Lexie,' she said. 'Especially when there's work to do.'

'And there's always work,' Lexie sighed. 'So how may a woman ever find time for feminine indulgences?' But her eyes were bright.

Shawneen, who had disarmed the others,

half-lifted the shotgun.

'Reckon the best way's to kill the varmints,' he said. 'They got it coming.'

Irons checked the gesture, making his voice even, though his legs were hard put to hold the reeling earth steady.

'We can't murder them,' he protested.

'I could do a dang good job tryin',' Shawneen insisted. 'Been plenty killin's hereabouts prior, and 'll be plenty more. Best cure for an itchin' foot I ever knowed.'

'Tie them up,' Irons ordered.

'They must o' hit a clip that addled yore brains,' Shawneen grumbled, but proceeded to obey orders with a thoroughgoing enjoyment, making sure that the bonds were tight. Rowena watched with increased horror. She had just recognized one of the quartet—the man who had handed the letter to her on board the packet.

Quint! The implications were clear. But no one was noticing her.

'This is a dang sight better'n you flea-bitten coyotes deserve,' Shawneen assured the prisoners as he worked. 'I reckon you'll get loose again, more's the pity. But you ornery coots'll be well advised to swaller yore cuds an' stay put. Do I ever sight ary one o' you over my rifle bar'l ag'in, I sure won't be able to control my finger, an' that's a promise.'

Irons remained erect, pausing long enough to help himself to the tent. But outside, even in the clean air, he could barely keep going. He was badly used up, and the women aided him, on either side. He mumbled a word of thanks.

'You folks—showed up just in time.'

'The credit goes to Aunt Lexie,' Rowena murmured. Softness threaded her voice, rounded her lips. 'She was on the street and saw you off this way, going into that house. When you didn't come out again she grew worried. So we came to have a look, guided by the screeching. Shawneen insisted that we should go armed.'

'Allers go with a gun, or a handful of 'em if you can,' Shawneen snorted. 'But we're sure storin' up trouble for ourselves, leavin' them mules to bray. It's dark enough, I could take 'em outside the town if you'd like it better.'

'Forget them,' Irons insisted. 'If you're so worried, we'll start travelin' now and leave them behind.'

'Which wouldn't be a bad notion,' Shawneen conceded. 'Only that the ol' hoss ain't fittin' to do no travelin' tonight.'

Irons slumped between the women, out on his feet. Shawneen slung him across his own shoulder and strode disgustedly ahead.

''Tain't nothin' to worry about,' he assured Rowena. 'I've seen him twice as bad off an' he shed it like a snake does its skin. He's tough. Mountain men have to be ornery as a grizzly b'ar and as thickheaded as a buffaler, an' next to Kit Carson he's the hardest to kill I ever seen. Give him a dose o' whiskey and a few hours' sleep an' he'll be rarin'.'

There was scant sleep in the calico room that night. The women watched over Irons, doctoring his hurts and, at the insistence of Shawneen and against their better judgment, giving him a drink of whiskey. Liquor, the old trapper declared, was the sure cure-all for whatever ailed a mountain man.

Irons was feverish, lightheaded. He'd taken terrific punishment, and even his constitution could not throw off the effects in a hurry. After midnight he slept fitfully, then awoke at that hour before dawn when the night is at its most silent. A few weeks later it would resound to bird-song, but that season was just ahead, and even the turbulence of this border town had subsided. This was like the prairie or the mountains—country where a man might be alone.

He was in no condition for retrospection or enjoyment. The fever burned brighter, and when Rowena brought him a drink of water it scarcely drove the phantoms from his mind. Striving grimly to keep a hold on reality, he talked, and because he was grateful as well as lightheaded, he told her why he was heading for the Green River and Rendezvous; of the break in beaver in far-off Europe, and the attendant ruin which that news could hold. Ruin for the thousands whose livelihood was tied, directly or indirectly, to the dam-builders of ten thousand streams.

Rowena sat beside him in the darkness, listening wide-eyed, all thought of sleep banished. So this was the news for which men were willing to murder—she had seen all too clearly that it was the reason for the attack upon him this evening. This was the work of Sanderson Parks, and she felt strong revulsion for the man and his methods. She half-wished that Irons had not feverishly babbled the secret.

Possessing it, she was faced with a grave responsibility. She had given her promise regarding this matter, but the brutality of the attack upon Irons, the way in which these men had planned to torture him, altered everything. Irons' explanation of Peter Burley's foresight and the ruin which he faced also shed new light on the whole matter. She had liked gruff, forthright Peter Burley—and she liked Peter Irons.

Reminding herself that this was a rough land did no good. There was but one certainty to cling to: she was going to the rendezvous to marry Paul Higginson, and he, too, faced ruin unless she helped him.

But every argument was confusion. She was troubled and uncertain when Irons, clutching her hand and seeming to find comfort in its touch, dozed off. Presently she slept from sheer weariness. Sunlight was in the room when the complaining voice of Shawneen roused them.

'You folks going to snooze all day?' he demanded. 'We shoulda been gone hours ago. The grass'll be knee-deep where they held the rendezvous, time we get there at this rate.'

Irons started guiltily and sat up, then, discovering where he had spent the night, went with Shawneen while Rowena and her aunt completed their toilet. His eyes were keen again, and he was quick to sense the purring complacency in Shawneen, despite his complaints.

'You sneaked back to that cabin, last night,' he charged.

'Well, an' why not?' Shawneen countered. 'They had it comin'.' He turned back the flap of his pouch, revealing a trophy, and grinned broadly as he closed it.

'They won't be doggin' our trail now,' he said. 'I found them critters clawin' to get loose, kinda suspicious I might circle on my trail, but I'd tied them to last. It didn't take much persuadin'—one was ready to yelp about the others to save his own skin. All three j'ined in assertin' it was that mule Zeb had done for Hooker, and I couldn't let that pass, now could I? And an example was what they needed. They won't foller us.'

Irons did not upbraid him. Having been a mountain man himself, he understood their point of view, and this was simple justice.

Shawneen had made concessions. Ordinarily he'd have dealt with all four alike, rather than allowing any to live. Now, out of deference for the women, he kept his trophy hidden. He'd lived so long among Indians that many of their ways were his, and he took as keen and childlike a delight in the scalp of an enemy.

This salutary lesson probably would frighten the trio off, where otherwise they would have been at their heels.

In the back of Irons' mind was an uneasy, half-remembered vision of the feverish night and a loose tongue, and of this he complained once the four of them were in the saddle and across the Blue.

'I must have been out of my head last night,' he said. 'I have a vague recollection. If—if I was garrulous or otherwise made a nuisance of myself, Rowena, I hope you will excuse it. It was the fever and, I think, a drink of whiskey those fellows poured down my throat. Whiskey always has that effect on me. I never could abide the stuff.'

'Your conduct was beyond reproach,' Rowena assured him, and fixed a stern eye on Shawneen, who avoided her gaze. 'Didn't you assure us that whiskey was a cure-all for any mountain man?' she demanded.

'Well, an' so 'tis,' Shawneen insisted. 'Leastways, for most. Pete there, he's 'bout the only hoss I ever saw can't hold likker. But

52

in some ways he ain't a proper mountain man.'

'Now what do you have to say to *that* charge, Mr. Irons?' Rowena demanded with mock severity.

Irons grinned. 'I guess I'll have to plead guilty,' he confessed. 'It's my early training, back East.'

'He had a lot of schoolin',' Shawneen cackled. 'Said he was all set for college 'fore his feet got to itchin'. College! An' in some ways he never did outgrow it.'

Rowena eyed Irons with new interest. He made no comment, and, the others relapsing into silence, she surveyed the surrounding country with approval. With Wayne City and Independence behind, the Blue at their backs, it was a wide, free land. A well-marked trail led into the northwest, and this they would follow to the Platte. It was a good day to be alive.

Both she and Lexie had done considerable riding at St. Louis, to toughen themselves for the trip. Rowena was pleased and amused to observe that she and her aunt were the equals of Irons at horsemanship, and considerably better then Shawneen, who was not exactly graceful in a saddle. He grinned wryly and admitted it.

'I ain't what you'd call right a home on a hoss's back,' he confessed. 'I was brung up to use my own laigs—shanks' hosses. Always

53

feel better when I'm doin' it, too. Run ahead of a bunch of howlin' Injuns most of a day, once. But I can make out this way when I have to. You wimmin ride good,' he added with grudging respect.

'We make out,' Rowena agreed, and let it go at that.

Thinking back, Irons was certain that he must have told Rowena the real reason for this trip, during that period of lightheadedness caused half by fever and half by whiskey. But he was not regretful. She was going with them, and for that, despite the hazards of the trail, he was glad. Viewing her, the sun in her hair, the joy of living in her eyes, he was certain that the secret was in good keeping.

His manner, in the days that followed, assured Rowena that he placed full trust in her. Irons was a mountain man, but her first intuition had been right. He was a gentleman, and the thought that she was making use of him to selfish ends was in danger of spoiling all enjoyment in the journey.

That she might be falling in love with him she refused to consider. She was already in love with another man, pledged to marry him, so any other notion was unthinkable. Parks had been right when he said that her duty lay to the man who was to be her husband. Every authority, scriptural and secular, supported that theory, and she clung to it desperately.

But that Irons might be falling in love with her she could not doubt, and it troubled her increasingly. Having traveled widely, she observed with penetration. It was no good to tell herself that Irons was merely being polite, even chivalrous, after she had thrust herself upon him for protection. When that was said, much was left to say.

The tent was only one evidence of his thoughtfulness. Shawneen had given it an initial treatment, spreading it across an anthill the first day.

'They like such fodder,' he explained. 'But they'll clean it up good. Won't miss nothin' that crawls nor hops.'

Well-aired, it had lost the taint of former surroundings, and at night it added greatly to the comfort and privacy of Lexie and herself.

Irons and Shawneen rolled in blankets beside the evening fire and wanted nothing better. Even when storm swept the land, they did not suffer. A few minutes' dexterous work and they had a lean-to shelter which they insisted was ample.

North and west! The words had a flavor of magic, matched by the land. It rolled endlessly to the horizon, always seeming larger beyond the skyline. Time ceased to have meaning, though they wasted none.

'This is a picnic, so far,' Shawneen grunted, and prophesied darkly. 'We're havin' too good a run o' luck. Makes this ol' hoss spooky. It won't last.'

He was an irreconcilable, who tolerated women on the journey because Irons insisted. Whether he worshipped deity or not, Rowena was doubtful, but that to him Irons was almost a god there was small doubt. But coupled with stubborn loyalty was an equally strong refusal to change his mind.

He refused to admit that the women wouldn't cause trouble, or that the idea wasn't wrong. Even the fact that both could outride him, that they remained cheerful under all circumstances, could not change him. They were ready to put as many hours on the trail as the men, and their cooking was a vast improvement over his own efforts. His attitude was that it was all a mistake, to be suffered as other hardships must be endured.

They were well away from the last taint of civilization when the weather changed. The sun had risen, warm with promise. An hour later it was displaced by a gray haze which drew in the horizon like a vague threat. In another fifteen minutes, taking no regard to the calendar, snow was spitting, and presently a full-fledged blizzard was upon them.

They kept grimly on until it became too great a chore, then made camp. In the untimely darkness preceding the usual hour of night, Lexie, heading for the near-by stream and a bucket of water, found to her

56

dismay that she had missed the creek. She turned about, but the camp fire and its light had vanished. When she called, choking down a feeling of hysteria that lumped in her throat, no answer came.

It was bewildering how quickly a friendly place could become hostile wilderness. At sunrise the sky had been high, the land areach to wide horizons. Now sky touched earth, the world drawn in, and storm beat with icy fists.

'Shawneen or Irons wouldn't be worried by this,' Lexie assured herself, and strove to think, to keep her mind a reasoning machine. 'The trouble is, I'm what Shawneen says I am—just a troublemaking woman! And when you start thinking such thoughts, you're getting panicky, which won't do at all.'

It was almost too dark to see, but she might follow her own tracks back to safety. The trouble was that already they were snow-filled, smeared over by the wind.

Though not far from camp, Lexie had no idea in which direction it lay. By moving she might wander farther, yet she dared not stand still. She walked, calling, but only the wind shrieked back.

Then a darker blur loomed and Shawneen was beside her, disapproval in face and voice.

'You better be gettin' back to camp, ma'am,' he said. 'Kind of risky, foolin' around in such weather.'

'I was lost, Shawneen,' Lexie confessed, and in her relief she was close to tears. 'I was never so glad to see anyone in my life.'

'Calc'lated you'd got mixed up,' he grunted. 'You been backtrackin' the way we come today, fast as you could go.'

CHAPTER FIVE

By morning the storm had cleared, leaving half a foot of snow on the ground, most of which melted during the day. Flowers shouldered it aside, patches of grass sprang green. Irons, viewing the wide sweep of land, saw houses and farms, and voiced his dream. Shawneen grunted disbelief, and Rowena saw not only the land but the man through new eyes.

I never should have come—not with him, she thought bleakly, and wondered anew where duty lay. But it was still a long way to journey's end.

Irons beguiled the days with accounts, not of his own exploits, but of others'; how the trappers lived; the tedium of cold months, when to assure a fair catch a man must be constantly on the move, regardless of weather; the perils of fang and claw, storm and snow-slide, unfriendly nature and hostile man—not all of whom were redskinned.

'A few years ago this country belonged to the Indians,' Irons added. 'Since they'd had it from the beginning of time, as you might say, you can't blame them too much for wanting to keep it. Now it's the mountain men who are taking over, getting the notion that it's theirs. But they'll soon be pushed aside by other newcomers. Homeseekers will be heading this way, just as they swarmed down into Kentucky and Ohio a few years ago.'

'Be a long time 'fore they ever get past the river,' Shawneen asserted confidently. 'This ol' hoss won't live to be bothered by them. This land's too big. It's beaver country, an' it'll keep on bein'—beaver an' buffaler.'

Irons, thinking of what was even now happening to beaver, shook his head. The frontier was changing, being pushed back at ever-increasing speed. He'd thought first that the break in beaver prices might reverse the trend, but it could have an opposite effect. If men couldn't make a living by trapping, they'd turn to more conventional means, which meant the pick and pan to some, saddle and cattle to others, but to the vast majority the plow and the hoe.

None of which was his concern. His job was to reach Rendezvous in time to save the Mountain Fur Company from disaster, and each mile added to his sense of depression. Most of the trappers who had ranged this territory during the winter were on the move ahead of them, but there were signs easily read, savvy to be gleaned. It had been a good fur year. The trappers had reaped a harvest of plews from every stream. Now they were heading for the gathering along the Green with what had always been sure, safe wealth, their hopes high.

They would not take kindly to the news that half their earnings were swept away with a breath. Nor would they look with favor on the man who brought such word. Europe, with its world of fashion, was shadowy and remote, never understood and scarcely considered. The companies that bought their plews had been the only tangible link with that world, and on them and their representatives would be visited the resentment—which, boiled down, would mean himself.

Considering these aspects, Irons was sorry that he'd allowed the women to come with them. There was sure to be trouble, and the trading place would be an ill one. He should have foreseen and made clear the risk. Instead, he had been so bemused that his mind had been in a trap.

Now he saw clearly. And now it was too late to make any changes.

Once they encountered buffalo. Other game was common. They reached the south branch of the Platte, dirty with flood. High water should have been past, but it was their luck to catch it at the crest. Surveying the bone in its teeth, Irons shook his head. He'd crossed rivers as bad, but never under such circumstances.

'This child's seen worse,' Shawneen asserted. 'I swum the Missouri once, an' it runnin' full of ice. Passel o' Injuns didn't leave no wide range o' choice.' His horse snorted and shied, distracting attention from the turgid swirl. Mud, partly dried, made a thin carpet back from the shore, where the water had reached. A scattering of willows rustled in the wind.

Half-hidden by these, a pair of feet protruded from among the brush, encased in well-worn moccasins. Above was equally ancient buckskin. The dead man lay, his neck twisted unpleasantly. Rowena stared down, repelled but fascinated, and wondered if she were going to be sick.

Irons soothed his skittish horse, eyes questing the riverbank and underbrush, while Shawneen, rising in the stirrups, sent his own glance roving back to the empty land they had crossed. Then it rested with uneasy question on the brushy, broken country across the river.

Dismounting, Irons discovered a second man, lying not far off. Both were white, and each had been scalped. Rowena found her voice in a hushed question.

'Indians?'

Irons shook his head. Shawneen, turning back from his survey, pointed to tracks in the mud.

'Them was made by shoes,' he said. 'An' Injuns don't wear shoes.'

'You mean *white* men have murdered and—and scalped them?' Lexie gasped. 'How horrible!'

''Tain't pretty,' Shawneen conceded. 'Bungling idiots,' he added with a snort. 'Might fool some, but never no mountain man.' He added, almost as an afterthought, 'You wimmin don't need to look.'

'We've already looked,' Rowena said practically. 'But why would white men do such a thing?'

'There might be two reasons,' Irons explained. 'Some turn renegade, and they're worse than Indians. In this case, I'd say these fellows had been waylaid for their fur. Likely they were heading for Rendezvous with a good catch. Then the men who scalped them did it to make it look like Indian work.'

Not far upstream, the river had gouged deeply into the overhang of the bank. They caved this down to make a common grave. It was the opinion of both Irons and Shawneen that the assault had happened the day before.

Finding the dead men had caused delay. Now the problem of crossing was thrust back at them.

'Reckon I better go first?' Shawneen

suggested, eyeing the flood. 'Kinda soak up some of the extra?'

'If it was whiskey, you might lower it,' Irons conceded. 'As it is, we'll try together.'

'Hold your guns high,' Shawneen instructed. 'Keep 'em dry. Never no tellin' what you'll find on t'other side a river. Even that fancy one might be better ef'n it ain't wet,' he added disdainfully, referring to Lexie's rifle.

Shawneen stuck to the old Kentucky rifle which he'd carried when first he crossed the Missouri, which had gone with him through varied tribulations. He swore that none of the newer weapons were in the same class when it came to trouble.

Irons favored a flintlock, .69 caliber, a smoothbore 1812 model. He, too, had become attached to this gun across the years, losing it a couple of times but always managing to get it back. Rowena's also was a .69, but shiny with newness, an officer's model with inclined brass pan, made by Nathan Starr of Middletown.

Lexie carried a Hall flintlock, which took a .52 caliber ball. Unlike the others, it was a breechloader, and Shawneen looked with dark suspicion on such newfangled ideas. If you got in a hurry, it would be sure to give trouble, so you might as well carry a club.

Lifting the gun from its case, Lexie held it in front of her, as the others were doing. If either woman had lost color at sight of the river, they had regained their composure and exhibited no hesitation as the horses moved reluctantly, making no attempt to disguise their dislike of what lay ahead.'

Ordinarily the Platte was wide and shallow, but today it ran deep and savage. The current curled as it struck the horses' legs, frothed toward their shoulders. Then they were swimming. Irons and Shawneen slipped out of saddles, swimming below their horses, aiding them as much as possible. Irons advised against Rowena or Lexie trying it.

'You're both considerably lighter than we are, and your horses can manage.'

The water was icy. Sand swirled grittily, and by midstream it seemed to Rowena that she would never be warm again. The river spread wide beyond its banks, giving the illusion of unlimited expanse.

Irons, keeping close, cried a sharp warning. A shower of mist and rain swept the water, and out of the haze a monster rushed, a gigantic batting ram carried by the flood.

It was a pine, the trunk broken off close above the earth which once had held it, become a jagged pile driver. There was no chance to dodge or turn back. Rowena's horse was in its path. She had a confused glimpse, then it hit and her horse went down and under.

Desperately she flung herself out of the

saddle, the sweeping branches lashing, the sullen gray current dragging her down.

She grabbed a branch, and was heaved into the air as the tree turned with the swing of the current. Irons shouted and swung his horse, and she saw the frantic look on his face.

For a minute she could not understand his purpose, for his horse was heading downstream, keeping ahead, widening the distance between.

His first notion had been to push close, to try to free her from the mass of branches. As the squall passed, he saw a boulder thrusting above the current, and changed his plan.

Scarcely was he below it when the drifting tree struck the barrier. It poised, then started to swing broadside, shoved relentlessly by the flood. The impact jerked Rowena loose despite her frenzied clutch. She fell clear, and as she came to the surface, Irons was alongside, dragging her up beside him.

Momentarily the dam created by the tree eased the current. Then the pine swung loose, the end missing them by inches as it bucked and plunged in a new frenzy. Rowena's arms closed more tightly about Irons.

Moments later the horse found a footing. They moved as though through an endless waste, but gradually the water shallowed, the shore no longer receded. Ground, though far from dry, was like a sight of the promised land. They scrambled out among brush and a few scraggly trees, and an infinity of mud. There was no sign of Lexie or Shawneen.

★   ★   ★

Lexie crossed without mishap, Shawneen keeping close. It was a responsibility which he wouldn't willingly have shouldered, but having it, he did his reluctant best. Emerging, he peered about for sight of the others and shrugged resignedly. Mist and rain had blanketed them away. Now clumps of brush and trees made it impossible to see far.

'They'll turn up,' he said. 'You stay here, and I'll have a look.'

It was a pretty pass when a man had to be cumbered with a woman. With a squaw it was different. They looked after themselves and the work, and expected nothing else. Raised in such country, squaws were as good at getting along as the braves, and sometimes better. They didn't expect much of a man, nor ask for it.

He rounded a clump of brush and wished he hadn't. Squarely in his path stood a giant grizzly.

His horse reared and snorted, then, not waiting for Shawneen to decide, took the bit in its teeth and set out for somewhere else. With a grizzly big as two bears ought to be, and cranky as a sick Injun, the horse wasn't to be blamed. The bear must be fresh out of hibernation, hungry and mean, and it was on their trail like a mink after a rabbit.

The trouble was that no horse could outrun a grizzly, and it was folly to try. He couldn't tell that to the straining animal, but it hampered a man when he wanted to get a good shot. And even under handicaps, it was get one or wish he had.

The horse did right well for the first few jumps. Long enough for the grizzly to get unlimbered. After that it was no contest. Shawneen tried to swing and get a lead, but he'd never claimed to be a horseman, and bouncing on a moving object, trying to center on another, was ticklish business. In a case such as this you made mighty sure of your first shot, knowing there wouldn't be a second.

Still he figured he might have done all right if something else hadn't distracted his attention at the critical moment. It was Lexie, heading after him and straight for the bear, urging her reluctant horse to greater efforts, when its instinct was to run the other way. The sight was disconcerting. By the time he could blink, opportunity had gone, for the bear had caught up.

It came like a nightmare full grown, running so spread out that the usual humpbacked ridge of muscle flattened. It was as though it had found wings and unfolded them in its feet, rising off the ground and straight at him. Shawneen fired point-blank and knew he'd missed, but the bear didn't. Shawneen spilled from the saddle as the grizzly clawed the horse down.

He landed, rolling, trying to get straightened around, knowing it wasn't likely to be allowed. Get a silvertip mad and you had plain p'izen. But he managed to come to his knees, feeling where he carried his knife, and not finding it. The grizzly was swinging at him, big as a mountain.

All the sounds ringing in his head made it hard to sort out the blast of the rifle, and twice as hard to believe as the bear reared higher, paws flailing air, a sudden gush of red from its mouth. Then it came down, almost on top of him, like a tree falling. Where it hit it stayed.

Lexie was getting off her horse, but she didn't run to him. She stopped like any mountain man and reloaded, mighty fast. Not that there was the need. The grizzly was dead enough. Shawneen shook weakness out of his legs and looked at it, and then he looked at Lexie, and the words came hard.

'Yo're better'n a squaw,' he said. 'Better'n even a Crow woman for savvyin' what to do. Be danged ef'n you ain't.'

Those were the right words. Lexie had felt suddenly that she was going to faint. She bit her lip and giggled, and looked with amazement at the bear. Dead, it seemed twice as big, and she wondered how she'd managed. There had been no time to think, only the need for a shot, and making it sure.

Shawneen found his own rifle and picked it from the mud, but the horse didn't need finishing. The grizzly had tended to that. His knife was off a way, where it had spilled as he did. Mechanically he set about loosening the pack behind the saddle, half-torn off by the downward swipe of long claws. He was alive, but he'd cut a sorry figure, and they were a horse short, here in the middle of nowhere and in a hurry.

The news was worse when Irons and Rowena rejoined them. Two horses gone and some of their supplies. Shawneen grunted.

'Best build a fire an' dry out,' he suggested. A trapper got used to such, but a woman couldn't be expected to relish it, and they owed something to these women. That bear had looked mighty big and ugly, so huge it was a puzzle how he could miss his shot.

Irons started to nod, and checked the motion. He looked at another track, one Shawneen had missed. A shoe had made it, not long before.

'Maybe we'd better see who's around, before we make a smoke,' he decided, remembering the dead men on the opposite shore. Beyond the river the ground sloped up into easy breaks, partially wooded. The shots might have been heard, and this was chancy country.

The pack horses were safe, but Rowena chose to walk. It was warmer that way. The shower had passed, but clouds kept sullenly between them and the sun. A small stream hurried to join the river, and for the first time, beaver tracks were plain in the mud. Irons pointed in silence, and the girls saw a beaver peeling bark from a twig.

It turned its head and saw them, but exhibited no fear until a horse snorted impatiently. Then it dived for deep water, its tail slapping loud in signal, and the ripples widened to the bank.

They went on, making a mile and then another. Shawneen, watching Irons, knew that he had the smell of trouble in his nostrils. He reckoned his own were clogged, for he'd sure 'nough been fooled by that grizzly, and he didn't quite figure this other.

But there were mountain men and Mountain Men. Pete Irons was like an Indian, only better. Take Carson or Bridger and you had a man to match him. Mostly the others were poor imitations, and that included himself, and supplied the reason why he'd stuck with Irons, even in that hole of a town.

He'd helped get them into a fix to rile the heart of a man, two horses short and time wasting.

Irons halted and held up a hand.

Shawneen heard it, then—the distant sound of a gun, blowing against the wind. Other guns answered in an echo of trouble.

The next knoll was wooded, and from it they had a look. The guns were falling silent when they gained the crest, and one more chapter of ambush and death was all but written. Only this time it was a case of reverse English.

Horses ran riderless and men sprawled on the unyielding earth. Others crept from the brush of ambush and grabbed a single remaining fugitive, the last of the party that, striving to defend themselves, had made a poor job of it. Fighting, the survivor was overpowered. Shawneen swore under his breath.

'Injuns, as I'm a wanderin' child,' he gasped. 'But set on by white men! That's turnin' the tables.'

Irons nodded. 'I'm int'rested in seein' if those fellows wear boots!'

'Now that's a notion,' Shawneen conceded. 'Those that did the killin' t'other side the crick was white, too.'

The party disappeared over a hill, conquerors and captive, horses and booty. It was a couple of miles ahead, and they moved warily, though losing no time. There were three dead Indians, when they came to the scene of the attack, and all had been scalped. Shawneen grunted with amazement.

71

'Comanche! And a long trek off'n their range!' He gazed about critically, then in a hoarse whisper volunteered information which might have a bearing.

'Know where we are? Off beyond that next rise is the shack of Ol' Mule. Might be they're holed up there. Ol' Mule was crazy as a loon an' stubborn as a skunk,' he added. 'Figgered to *farm* in such a country!'

'A shack, eh?' Irons asked. 'How far?'

'A middlin' loud holler. Quarter of a mile.'

Rowena ventured a question. 'What happened to Mule?'

'Injuns parted his hair,' Shawneen said briefly. 'What there was of it.' He cocked his head like a bird. 'Somethin' funny.'

Irons nodded and led the way. They crested the slope, and the horses were below—half a dozen, hobbled and grazing, where the grass was green. Beyond, half-hidden by trees, was the cabin, its spindling poles weathered and warped. A sound came with recurring regularity, a faint but solid thud, like a hammer on wood, yet somehow different. A voice drifted on the wind.

'That was close, ol' hoss. But watch this'n!'

'Aw, I can beat the two of ye. I'll draw blood without scurcely cuttin' his hide.'

Now they could see, and Rowena's hand pressed hard against her mouth. There was open ground around the cabin, a natural clearing amid this wooded tract. Gathered here were the attackers of the recent ambush, three white men, though it required a second look to be sure that they were white. All of them wore shoes, instead of moccasins.

At their belts each man wore something else—new trophies, rawly fresh. Rowena's knuckles hurt beneath her teeth.

The captive Indian was little more than a boy, and he stood beside the cabin, his back to the logs. Mud chinking had fallen from between the timbers, leaving gaping cracks. Through these ropes had been passed, tying the Indian's arms, outspread to either side. In that position he was helpless.

His captors were engaged in a pastime at once skillful and ferocious. A long-bladed knife still quivered, point deep-buried in the wood, so close to the boy's left arm that a trickle of blood broke from the punctured skin. The last boast had been accurate.

The trio were taking turns, standing back a score of feet, throwing with calculated precision. Even to Rowena's untutored eyes it was apparent that these men were skillful performers with their chosen weapon.

Another knife sped like a shaft of light, and she stifled a cry, certain that the point must bury itself deep in the throat of the victim, who watched his tormentors and endured the thud of the blade without flinching. It quivered so close that the cold steel touched skin.

Another took his turn, and still Irons made no move. But their purpose could not be doubted. Striving to come closer each time, finally they would cut the boy to pieces. Irons shifted his rifle and moved forward, Shawneen at his heels.

His greeting, as the others swung, was disarmingly mild.

'Havin' fun?' he asked.

CHAPTER SIX

Irons stood with his feet bunched as if for a spring. Aside from that, he appeared relaxed and faintly contemptuous. Yet never had he seemed taller, more sure of himself. The trio regarded him uncertainly, suspicious as coyotes downwind to an alien scent. Coyote was too mild a word for this pack. To Rowena, all three appeared curiously alike despite physical differences. One wolf in a pack might be huge, as a club-footed man was among the three; another could be old and gray, while a third would drag an injured leg, but basically all were wolves.

A boot's deep imprint showed in the mud. Lexie's breath caught as she recognized the peculiar pattern of hobnails, the same as those smashed into the mud on the far shore of the river. She raised her eyes, and found others upon herself—a gaze like the beady stare of a vulture.

'Fun? Why, uh—yo're plumb c'rrect, mistah.' The wearer of the boots moistened his lips with an uneasy tongue. 'Didn't know we had comp'ny. You kind of snuck up on us, for a fact.'

He made as if to tug off a nondescript cap, his glance sidling toward the women, but checked in indecision. His face, which had gone a toad's belly yellow, flooded again with choleric color.

'We're kind of smellin' out,' Shawneen interpolated mildly. 'Found a couple of dead men t'other side the water, then we saw you ketch those Injuns. Seems like they hunt in pairs.' He gestured toward the tense captive. 'I'm purely surprised you took him alive.'

The spokesman reached a conclusion. One shoulder hunched, peaklike.

'We figgered it might be foxy,' he said. 'That bunch of hair-hunters been hangin' on our trail better'n a week. Our two pards disappeared, and we was pretty sure the redskins had rubbed them out. You say you found them t'other side the river? Now that proves it.

'Today, that bunch jumped us sudden, thinkin' they'd kotched me an' Jabe alone, but they miscalculated. Purely did, for a fact. Bart was off scoutin', and he snuck up behind 'em, after which it was a leetle to our favor. We managed to grab this hoss-stealer alive, an' been workin' on him to loosen his tongue about our pards.'

Irons' rifle shifted. As if by accident, the muzzle now covered the trio.

'That's your story, eh? A week! Now we'll hear the Injun's side. What you got to say, boy?'

The Indian spat one word, contemptuously. 'Lies!'

Clubfoot started forward, but checked at Shawneen's gesture. His tongue was vitriolic.

'Why, you stinkin' snake, you—'

'Hold up!' Irons warned. Anger made a flat plane of his face. 'Go ahead,' he invited the captive. 'You're Comanche?'

'Yes, Comanche.' It was proud acknowledgment.

'Kind of off your range, ain't you?'

'All range Comanche. Travel where please.'

'These Injuns have sure got cocky since they stole white men's horses,' Jabe growled into a tangled beard.

'You seem to savvy English,' Irons murmured, disregarding the others. 'Go on, tell your story.'

'You ain't aimin' to listen to a stinkin' Injun against white men, are you?' Clubfoot protested.

Irons shrugged. 'Your story is as loose as the tracks of a dying buffalo. Now it's his turn.'

'Ride this way first time, today,' the boy explained. 'Never see 'um before. Not looking for trouble. They jump me an' my friends.' For an instant his face showed emotion. 'Not give us chance. Kill them, steal our horses. Think mebby we carry plews, try make me tell where to find them. Can't tell; we not trappers.'

His words were confirmation of the evidence already seen—that these were no true mountain men, but blundering tenderfeet.

''Tain't so,' the big man denied. 'I tell you they been trailin' us a week, waitin' for the chance to jump us, an' they bushwhacked our pards—'

'No kill their pards,' the Indian denied. 'Not know 'em.'

Clubfoot fingered the knife which he had slipped into its sheath. Rowena, transferring her gaze from the scalp so close to it, noticed that the handle was painted red.

Shawneen had moved off, questing like a hound. He eased around the corner of the shack, and contempt threaded his voice.

'Some mules never learn that brayin' won't cover up a set o' tracks,' he said disgustedly. 'There's a couple bundles o' plews stashed inside. White men's plews—but they been busted open, then repacked mighty careless.'

Irons had been certain from the beginning,

but such evidence was indisputable. Trappers on their way to the rendezvous transported their fur in the best possible condition. The bundles must have belonged to the pair across the river. Only thieves would find it necessary to break open the packs, so that they would know the tally when it came time to trade.

Rowena saw the trouble in Irons' face, and knew that once again it was because of Lexie and herself. This was a land without law. Each man made his own, carried it with him, and the measure of it was also the measure of his own safety. Retribution must be the price of crime, justice dealt swiftly. If Irons and Shawneen were alone, there would be no question and no problem.

Because of their presence the simple was made complex. It even became a noose to throttle. Irons made his decision.

'Like the Injun says, you're lying. Your tracks were alongside those dead men. We should treat you the same—but we'll give you a chance. You can head out, afoot. Don't be in a hurry to swing back!'

They stared, uncertain, doubtful of their luck.

Jabe whined, 'But we'll starve. We won't have a chance without guns or grub.'

'What chance did you give the others?' Irons asked contemptuously. 'It would serve you right. But we'll leave guns and grub in the cabin. But right now, you'd better travel before I change my mind.'

'We'll go, since we ain't got no choice,' Clubfoot agreed. 'But one o' these days, this knife o' mine—' He left the threat unfinished.

They moved away, sullenly at first, then scuttling as though fearful that Irons would change his mind. Shawneen watched with glum resignation, and cut the Indian loose. Freed of the support of the ropes, the boy staggered and clutched at the edge of the cabin to steady himself.

'Why, he's hurt,' Rowena exclaimed, and caught him. 'He's been shot.'

It was a bullet hole, high up, through his right shoulder. The lead had made a small clean wound, both where it entered and went out, without much bleeding.

He submitted passively as the women cleansed the wound and bandaged it, and Rowena looked anxiously at Irons.

'He needs good care and nursing, and should be quiet for several days.' She frowned. 'I don't know what to do.'

The boy solved that by walking toward one of the horses.

'I go now,' he said with dignity. 'Tall Man not forget.' He sprang on the horse, more clumsily than he had intended, and boyish mortification crossed his face at this manifestation of weakness.

'They took my gun,' he added, on a note of question.

Irons brought a rifle and handed it up.

'Take an extra horse,' he invited. 'The plews too, if you like.'

Tall Man shook his head, and in that moment justified his name.

'Skins not mine,' he denied. His glance roved, calculatingly, toward the break where the trio had disappeared, but he swung his horse in another direction. With his good arm he lifted the rifle in salutation, then was gone.

'He should have rested,' Rowena said again. 'It was a bad wound.'

'He's an Indian,' Irons reminded her. 'We'd better be travelin', too.'

Rowena watched Irons increasingly as they journeyed. Just as Tall Man was appropriate for the Indian, so, it seemed to her, did Irons live up to his name. Yet that was not quite accurate. He was strong, in a land where strength counted, but he could bend like tempered steel. And behind the strength there was a tenderness like the green shoot of a willow.

The sun more than kept pace with them. The days had lengthened into weeks, and these spelled out the miles of a land vast and primitive. Mountains rose out of the west, and far to the north they sighted sky-piercing peaks, deep blue with tips of white, like magpies perched high.

Where they crossed the divide the trail was easy, and Rowena found the mountains disappointing. It was as though, reaching for the sun, she had been given a candle. Here the Rockies were in gentler mood than where they bestrode a continent to the north.

But such matters were minor. Her greatest concern was with herself and this man who rode beside her.

That he loved her she had long since ceased to doubt. Not that he had spoken in any direct way, but there was no need. When the sun is all about, it is impossible to miss its warmth and brightness. Irons' love was as strongly compelling, as pervading, and—if she dared let it—would be as warming.

She was promised to another man, and journeying to marry him. A promise given was a pledge which might not be broken. But somewhere along the way this trip had lost its high expectation.

Soberly she took her resolution. She must make Irons hate her—there was no other way. If he found her cheap and undesirable, his hurt would be lessened. It would be easier if she could hate him in turn. Now, when she turned the knife, the greater wound would be in her own heart.

Causing him to hate her would be simple, for she had only to deliver her message to Paul Higginson. Beyond that step, she refused to think. Duty came first, no matter what the cost. It was strange that duty and love should become so inextricably combined with emotions completely alien.

They topped a last easy slope and came in sight of the big camp at midafternoon of a cloudy day. The Green rolled out of the north, wide and shallow, then, gathering itself between frowning banks, made haste as though it had caught the taint of evil.

The cottonwood leaves held the soft green of early summer, and willows fringing the creeks were rash with new growth. Tepees had the look of pointed mushrooms, sprung up overnight in haphazard profusion. Shawneen, sucking in a deep breath, was at once enraptured and troubled.

'There she be,' he pronounced, and his smile gave way to a twisted scowl. 'Bigger'n usual, from the looks. And twice as many Injuns.'

Rowena guessed what he meant. Normally a large encampment would be welcomed by the traders. The more men, the more fur. But this year extra plews and an overabundance of trappers was only a piling-on of trouble.

★   ★   ★

Legs spread apart in one of the larger tepees, Paul Higginson wiped the lather from his razor, making faces at himself in a small metal mirror suspended from a pole. He studied his reflection, pleased. The lean angle of jaw tipped handsomely to match the aquiline curve of nose, faintly suggestive of an eagle's beak. His skin was fresh and smooth, healthily tanned but without a leathery appearance. He turned in high good humor to grin at his companion.

Cross-legged on a thick pile of buffalo robes, the girl Running Fawn watched with an amused air of mingled interest and proprietary tolerance. As Pawnees went, she was tall, as lithely graceful as the white aspens along the riverbank. Her eyes had a quality of dipped liquid, still uncooled, a soft shimmer of warmth like mist. They darkened with a quick displeasure echoed in Higginson's own as a figure in buckskin thrust aside the flaps.

The intruder was a wizened man, for all his youthfulness. All the sap of life seemed squeezed out, the glow drained from saddened eyes. Only for a moment, as they fixed on Running Fawn, did they brighten.

'I got news, Hig,' he announced mournfully. 'Some which you ain't going to cotton to.'

'What do you mean?' Higginson, having wiped the blade, folded the razor carefully, his eyes suddenly wary.

'There's a passel o' riders headin' for camp,' Yosemite said. 'They're a couple miles off yet. Four or 'em. Looks to be two men an' a pair o' wimmin.'

'Well?' Impatience rasped Higginson's voice. 'What's so unusual about a couple of trappers and their squaws?'

The bearer of tidings wiped tobacco stain from his lips with the backward sweep of a hairy hand. His voice took on a sly undercurrent at variance with the meekness of his face.

'These ain't squaws,' Yosemite cackled. 'Leastways, not the usual run. Mebby you rec'lect, you took me along when you went East last year, Hig? Seein' them swarmin' cities an' suchlike?'

'And you were more of a nuisance than you were worth, the same as you are here,' Higginson snapped. 'What about it?'

'On'y that one of these gals ridin' in now is the one you was sweet on back in Gin'ral Jackson's town. She's Rowena McCoy, or I'm a dehorned buffalo.' His glance slid to Running Fawn and away, and he tasted the words lingeringly. 'Must be she's comin' to marry you, like she said she'd do.'

'What's that?' Higginson's jaw sagged in sharp unbelief, while Running Fawn stirred tensely. His teeth snapped. 'You're crazy, man!'

'Them with her,' Yosemite went on, unperturbed, 'are ol' Shawneen an' Pete Irons from St. Louis. Can't fool me on that pair!'

'The devil!' Higginson's calm was in danger of breaking. Frantically he attempted to assess the meaning of the news, while Yosemite surveyed him with a mournful aspect which hardly concealed the triumphant mockery beneath.

Yosemite turned and disappeared, allowing the flaps of the tepee to drop in place. Instantly, Running Fawn was on her feet and across the intervening space. Her eyes had the sheen of a she-wolf's.

'What is this?' she demanded. 'What white squaw comes to marry you? I will kill her!'

Higginson's face twisted in the answering hint of a snarl. Rarely had any news so shocked him, but already his mind was surveying and assessing. His fingers clawed urgently at the girl's shoulders.

'I don't know what it is, Running Fawn, except that it's a mistake,' he said quickly. 'You know the tongue of Yosemite, which is twisted and malicious. But it will be better for you to return to your father's tepee for the present. I must learn what this means.'

In her quick movement he sensed trouble. With an ordinary squaw, one had but to command to be obeyed, meekly and without question. It was Running Fawn's unlikeness to the run of her red sisters that had first attracted him, a flaming spirit shining through flesh which could scarce encompass the fire. Her answer was instant and positive.

'No! I am your woman. You buy me with much tobacco, many fine presents. I leave my father's tepee to dwell in yours. Here I remain. I am no tame squaw to be cast aside for another!'

She spoke in her own tongue, in whose use Higginson was well-schooled. Running Fawn possessed the immutable dignity of her race, the strong pride found usually only in a proved warrior or chief. Not for her the submissive role of the squaw, though on occasion she could be tender. All these traits had drawn him, but in this moment they stirred his anger.

'You've got to go,' he insisted. 'Just for a while, until I get this straightened out. I'm not casting you off. It's only that I've got to have time.'

Running Fawn was unmoved. A woman's realistic wisdom looked out of her dark eyes.

'Time for her,' she mocked. 'If she comes to marry you, then you would have no more time for me. But I am not like the winter's campground when spring comes, to be forever abandoned.'

Higginson cursed Yosemite under his breath, hating the man for a loose-tongued fool, though it was more than that. There had been a measure of spite in the warning. Yosemite had aspired to the chief's daughter. In fact, he had all but concluded a deal before Higginson had become interested, and with her consent. Even now he would take her off Higginson's hands quickly enough, but the matter was not so easy of solution. That was of the past, and the mere suggestion would fan Running Fawn's fury like wind behind a prairie fire.

It was no accident that Parks and Higginson were partners. One was a field man, the other city-bred and by nature a handler of detail. They complemented each other, running the same trail like two Indians leaving a single set of tracks. Ambition and greed and lack of scruple had drawn them together.

Whatever the cost, Higginson knew that he must appear well in the eyes of Rowena. He'd never taken seriously her promise to come to this wild frontier and marry him. It was a crazy notion, but since she was here, she would expect some responsiveness on his part.

He must appease her, and do whatever she wanted, because she was the stepping-stone to everything he desired. One day he would leave this raw land behind forever. When that time came, Rowena had what he lacked—social position, wealth.

Running Fawn's smile was mocking. 'So this white squaw, who is to marry you, journeys with other white men,' she murmured.

Higginson swiveled to a halt. Momentarily, that aspect had escaped him. But if Rowena was with Irons, then she must have come with him all the way from St. Louis. At the thought, a surge of jealousy swung his rage into new channels.

He spoke quickly, the words making a pattern almost before his mind had formed the scheme.

'Running Fawn, I need your help.' This was the right appeal. 'You can do what is needed—perfectly. You know how to kiss as a white woman does—better than most! Do this for me, and I'll do anything for you!'

He explained what he wanted, and Running Fawn's eyes grew secret, clouded over like those of a hawk. He was unable to fathom the thoughts behind that mask, but so long as she was willing, that was all that mattered. After a question or so, she turned and hastened out.

Half-concealed behind a clump of brush, Higginson saw her run to meet the newcomers, and heard her quick, keening cry of joy, so well done that it would have fooled even himself. For just an instant her gaze swerved, missing no detail of the younger white woman or the beauty in her face. In that instant Running Fawn was wholly primitive.

A lithe leap carried her up, on to Irons' horse, into the saddle in front of him. Her arms went about him.

'Pete! Ah, it has been so long—so-o long, but at las' you come back to me!'

CHAPTER SEVEN

Running Fawn's tempestuous greeting caught Irons off-guard. For a moment he submitted dazedly, then, catching a glimpse of Rowena's face, he reacted in dismay. The violence of his effort to free himself of her embrace almost sent the Indian girl toppling, but she saved herself nimbly, drawing back to stare at him. Hurt filled her eyes.

'Pete!' she gasped. 'You not love me any more? You forget Running Fawn, who love you so-o much? Or'—her eyes were twin lava pools as they swung to Rowena—'maybe you find someone in my place?'

Higginson chuckled under his breath. The little devil was a born actress, possessed of sufficient native cruelty to enjoy the part. That had been pure inspiration, sticking her on to Irons. He'd always hated the man, and his coming now could only mean trouble. Since Rowena had trusted herself to his guidance, it was mere insurance now to make him appear despicable. Running Fawn was seeing to that.

'I don't know what you're talking about,' Irons protested. 'You're all mixed up. I never saw you before in my life.'

Running Fawn's eyes brightened with a hint of mischief. That might be true, on his part, but she at least had seen him before. Two summers ago, from the shelter of her father's tepee, she had watched wistfully as he passed. He had looked at her, and she had dropped her eyes and smiled her prettiest, angrily aware in that same moment that he didn't see her—not as a woman. Now a measure of revenge was sweet.

'You say that, to Running Fawn?' Her voice broke piteously, and her eyes rounded upon the shocked face of Rowena. 'Because of white squaw you forget me? Now my heart is caught in the jaws of a wolf!'

She slipped stumblingly to the ground and fled without a backward glance. Irons sat stunned, hardly certain of what had happened to him. In a space of seconds, home-coming had been turned into nightmare, and he felt like a heel. Then he saw the hurt and incredulity in Rowena's eyes.

'The little devil!' he muttered. One thing was certain: there was no past between them, and the Indian girl had acted her part too well for chance. But his words, blended of anger and admiration, were unfortunate. Rowena's glance raked him scornfully.

'Call me a catamount!' Shawneen muttered, and added thoughtfully, 'Man, was she purty!'

Higginson chose that moment for his own entrance. He came, apparently breathless with haste, excitement booming through his voice.

'Rowena! It is you! I couldn't believe my eyes when I saw you coming!'

She turned to him with relief, though she had increasingly dreaded this moment as the miles lessened. Abruptly the way was clear to despise Irons.

'Paul!' she sighed, and was in his arms. 'Oh, Paul, it's so good to see you!'

Irons watched in shocked unbelief. Never, by word or suggestion, had she admitted knowing Paul Higginson, yet now she was snatched off her horse and into his embrace.

Higginson held her tightly, making no effort to hide his elation. Rowena's reaction to Running Fawn's byplay had confirmed his fears and sharpened his jealousy. Getting Running Fawn to stage the scene had been a good hunch. Even more to the point, he could now play his part with no danger of interruption from the Pawnee girl. After the public display which she had just put on, she could not break in without making a laughingstock of herself, an object of ribald glee before her red sisters.

Running Fawn had checked her flight behind the first clump of brush, and turned to watch. Higginson had tricked her into a position which left her weaponless. Boldly, he plunged all the way.

'I never dared believe that you would come, Rowena,' he said. 'I knew you were an

91

extraordinary woman, but that you would make such a journey to join me—I really didn't suppose you would! But you have!'

'I'm here, Paul,' she agreed and, because of the hurt that still twisted at her heart, added proudly, 'I said I'd marry you at Rendezvous. Here I am.'

This was the trappers' section of the camp, and a crowd of the mountain men were collecting, drawn by curiosity. Awe held them silent, even from exchanging greetings with these two who were old friends of many.

Irons' rage exploded into action. Abruptly he pulled his horse around, gesturing savagely to Shawneen to leave the pack animals, and rode off without a backward glance. His mind had been busy with plans for the comfort of the women, but that had been taken out of his hands. Hurt was sharp as a knife cut, and his impulse was to get away. His fury mounted as he realized that he was the victim of a double trick, from which there could be no escape.

Rowena looked up to see the bitter straightness of his back, and only the memory of the Indian girl kept her from crying out. Pride came to her rescue. She had acknowledged that she was here to marry Paul Higginson, and how these others would gibe if she called after a man claimed by a squaw! She turned numbly.

'I'm tired, Paul,' she whispered.

Irons' glance sharpened as he rode. He'd

been a man bemused these latter days, and suddenly he knew himself for a fool. Shawneen had really been guide across the mountains and down these western slopes to the river. It was his unsleeping vigilance which had kept them from blundering more than once.

Sight of the camp, sprawling on the two sides of the Green, had been a hope fulfilled. Now he viewed it with a more seeing eye. It was of the pattern of other years, yet with a difference. He pulled up, studying the situation, not liking it.

'Seems to me there's a passel more of Indians than usual,' he observed.

'This child's been thinkin' the same,' Shawneen conceded, glad to avoid the subject uppermost in both their minds. Women were chancy critters, as he'd always contended, and he was a fool to be shocked or surprised. That was the nub of the matter—he was a fool, same as Irons.

'Twice as many tribes have got the itch for a snootful of whiskey, looks like,' he added. 'Which means twice as much hell.' His finger stabbed rangingly. 'There's Crow an' 'Pahoe, Big Bellies an' Sioux—an' that ain't a beginnin'. Looks like mighty near every tribe west o' the big river had sent a deppitation. Which adds up to too many. It's like you'd set your trap for a beaver an' ketched a bear.'

Irons nodded. Outwardly, at least, the
93

Indians were friendly, come here to trade, and, like the mountain men, to hold high revel. Whiskey was for the buying, if sufficient plews were offered. Higginson had assured them of liquor in years past. The Mountain, like the Hudson's Bay to the north, frowned on such methods, but Parks and Higginson had been their own law.

It would be a poor quality of liquor which they furnished, doctored and diluted, yet strong enough to slash like a scythe in a man's throat and thereafter drive him to frenzy. For the doubtful benefits of this fire water the Indians would sell their souls, and all lesser possessions—horses, robes, tepees, squaws.

Such a large gathering was another factor Irons hadn't counted on. It meant just so many more who would be sullenly angry when their wealth was sliced in half.

The trading ground was ahead, a generally open section midway between the white and the Indian portions of the camp. Preparations had been made for displaying goods and handling fur, but it was plain that not much actual trading had taken place. They were in time, but even that was a wry satisfaction.

Jim Hammond came out of an oversized tepee, attracted by the distant commotion, squinting against the sun from beneath a leveled hand. Then, his glance brightening with recognition, he waved and yelled. He walked with a limp, one foot dragging from an old injury, but after the first glance men forgot his foot, their gaze drawn higher. The calm blue of the sky had settled in his eyes; the sun of serene days was in his face.

'Well, call me a buffalo!' he ejaculated. 'Things ain't never so bad but what they can get worse, seems like! Howdy, Peter!' His grip matched Irons' name as the latter swung down from his horse. 'Howdy, Shawneen! What brings you two coons, when they ain't no sheriff to chase you?'

Irons grinned briefly at the welcome, but he wasted no time in palaver.

'You bought much fur, Jim?'

Hammond's eyes narrowed. 'Tradin's slow in startin'. But they're commencin' to warm up. Come tomorrow, I figger we'll be busy as a pup with his first set o' fleas.'

'Good.' The word could mean anything. 'Let's make medicine. Shawneen, you set up our camp.'

The rich smell of plews was close in the tepee, and Irons took a quick look. There were a few mink, dark and sleek, a pile two hands high of beaver, skins from some stream far to the north as their texture and color denoted. Three wolves, a pair of foxes. Nibblings.

Tobacco, bolts of cloth, and other odors combined to make a remembered, pleasant fragrance. Hammond's clerk slipped out quietly at a gesture.

'You fresh out from St. Louis, Pete?'

'Straight and fast as we could travel. Burley sent me.'

Hammond understood. Pete Burley had been expectant of news from overseas. Hammond could tell that it was bad.

'Must have taken somethin' to pry you loose.'

'This could mean ruin for Burley, so of course I came. They've quit usin' beaver in their hats over in Europe. Which has clawed the price right out from under. We'll still buy, of course—but cut the price in half. Even at that, it's a gamble.'

Hammond was silent, while the breath went out of him. He'd been afraid of this, but in no such degree. Half! That was the same as telling a man that all his profit was wiped away; that the added toil in bitter weather, the risks of a winter spent among hostiles, was all for nought. Here at Rendezvous the Indians were outwardly friendly, but alone in the hills a man never knew. With no one to see, most any brave was apt to prize your plew higher than a beaver's, and such peril was with a man always, waking or sleeping. For that, you needed a bit of a profit, particularly when it came to the rendezvous, to the big holiday of the long year.

To be told that the profit was gone, half a year wasted, even existence cut thin—that was bad. The mountain men wouldn't like it.

And the Indians—

It was strange, but even while you feared and hated, because of the unending distrust, still you sort of came to like them, to see things more or less with their eyes.

If they hated and feared and killed when the chance offered, it was natural enough. Often there was cause. An Indian's life was hard, always balanced on the threshold of existence, becoming doubly precarious since the white men had upset the ancient balance. You could hardly blame them, any more than a white man, for wanting something extra now and then, and expecting to get it when they sold their plews.

They, too, would be enraged at the price cut. Any way you looked at it, this was bad.

'How do we handle it?' he asked.

'We'll go slow till Higginson loads up at the old price—then do the best we can.'

Hammond scratched his ear, his gaze fixed on the distant snow peaks.

'May be kind of hard to make him take the lead. He'll be suspicious, with you comin' in. Up to now, he ain't been buyin' much, nor committin' himself.'

Until now, Irons' thought had been mostly for Sanderson Parks. He disliked Higginson, and with cause, but until today the man hadn't really mattered. It was Parks whom Burley wanted to see put out of business, and considering the way he did business, that was understandable, a feeling shared.

But the events of the past hour had changed all that. Higginson was partner to Parks, and Irons suddenly had a real reason to hate. If he could be busted wide open, so much the better. If Rowena still wanted to marry the man—

He closed his mind on that, and fell to discussing details with Hammond. Difficult or not, all that could be done was to play along for a few days, buying as little as possible, being finicky about the quality of fur, but with no abrupt change in price.

'That way, they'll think we're hard to suit. After about so much stalling, the trappers will get impatient. When they do, they'll sell to Higginson. That's fine. The more he takes away from them at the old price, the better.'

Hammond nodded thoughtfully.

'Yeah. Sounds like the best way to work it.'

'When the hook is in him will be soon enough to let out the news,' Irons added, and looked up as Shawneen jerked back the tent flap.

The sun had made a wide dip as they talked, the day growing old. Some of its age seemed transplanted to Shawneen's usually impassive face.

'Best be ready for trouble,' he warned. 'There's been dirty work.' His face twisted at thought of how the news had been carried. 'The story's out and spreadin'. Higginson's cut the price on plews—cut it in half!'

CHAPTER EIGHT

Rowena lost no time in telling Higginson what had brought Irons to Rendezvous, imparting the vital information which was more than half her own reason for coming. She talked while anger was still upon her, remembering Running Fawn and the shameless manner in which she had thrown herself at Irons. The old arguments, advanced by Parks and repeated over and over in her mind, had grown stale. But such conduct was justification. If that was the sort of man he was—

Higginson listened, as shocked as he was startled by the news. He had no reason to doubt it, for such men as Burley, Irons, and Parks were too shrewd to be imposed upon. But the implications were staggering.

There would be trouble, but nothing compared to the ruin which would have faced him had he lacked this information. He'd been set to gamble, to raise the price and outbid Hammond, and, by choking off the source of supply, force the Mountain out of business. If they met his bid, he'd bankrupt them.

Parks might not like his method, arguing

that they too could be ruined in the process. But a monopoly of plews would partly enable them to fix their own resale price. And when he returned, he could marry Rowena, and recoup temporary losses from her fortune...

Under changed conditions, that would have meant certain disaster. Then his mind rallied, setting to work on the problem. If he handled it right, he might be able to salvage something from the wreckage, to shift the onus on to Irons and the Mountain.

He thanked Rowena, fervently assuring her that she had saved him from ruin. Somewhat reassured, she went to the tent which had been set up, observing that it was pitched at a considerable distance from Higginson's tepee. That was strange, for there had been an open space close to his, and she had supposed that he would have her tent near by. But he had been strangely distraught—more, it seemed, then the news justified.

She sank down on a buffalo robe, refusing to meet her aunt's eyes as Lexie sought to make this abode as homelike as possible. There would be accusation in her aunt's face, but, anger blazing high again, she looked up.

'Don't look at me that way, Lexie. You knew all along why I was coming out here—to marry Paul!'

'Of course I knew,' Lexie agreed. 'But Mr. Irons did not. I could see no justification for your keeping it from him particularly when you, being no dunce, could see how he felt toward you. But to break it to him in such a manner—'

'How could I help it? Paul was there. And he had to know. Besides, he deserved it. You—you saw that shameless hussy!'

'I saw her,' Lexie agreed. 'I suppose you were watching *her*. I was looking at Mr. Irons.'

'I hope you enjoyed the spectacle!'

'That's unjust, Rowena. And particularly so to him. If you had observed him closely, you must have seen how utterly bewildered he was. And do you remember what he said? That she must be mixed up, because he had never seen her before?'

'That was for my benefit, I suppose,' Rowena said bitterly. 'He is the great Peter Irons, far above the common run of men—one who never looked at a squaw! But she knew *him* well enough!'

'She seemed to,' Lexie agreed reluctantly. 'Just the same, I prefer to judge him by what I've seen on the trail. I think you were needlessly cruel.'

Her conscience assured Rowena of the same. Both accusing voices served only to increase her anger. She leaped to her feet, thrust aside the flap of the tent, and stepped out into the evening.

The valley of the Green was a wide, easy slope, like an opened friendly hand. The

101

rising plumes of a hundred cook fires lifted; a hum of voices was intermingled with the playing of children and the barking of dogs. Though this was all new and strange, she could see that there were two separate camps—that of the mountain men on this far side of the river, which they had forded at a shallows. The Indians were on the opposite bank.

The tents and tepees of the trappers were pitched in careless disarray. Those of the Indians, she decided, were according to tribe, separate, but near and friendly as two dogs smelling noses. Except that the two were a pack.

Here the Green was not overly wide, confined at this point between sharp banks, running deep and swift. Someone had thrown a log across, to bridge the gap. It was not a good span, and normally she would have hesitated, but in her present mood Rowena walked across with scarcely a thought for what a slip might mean.

She wandered among the tepees, aware of squaws who watched in stolid lack of emotion, neither friendly nor hostile, and of younger women who smiled shyly. A few warriors glanced her way with carefully concealed interest and then looked beyond her. Suddenly she halted in unbelief.

The flaps of a large tepee were tied back, revealing a shadowy interior. In this doorway a lithely proportioned man squatted cross-legged. He wore a long black robe, and a clerical hat rested upon the thick darkness of his hair.

It was startling to see a priest in this remote camp, and doubly so against such a background. But that was nothing to the man himself. Rowena's breath threatened to choke her. She had seen that high-bred, imperious face with the thin-nostriled, aquiline nose too many times to doubt. The deep-set eyes, always lit with a faintly sardonic humor, could never be offset or hidden by any garment, however incongruous.

He had been watching, having discovered her long before she had seen him, and now he lifted a hand in easy salutation. His deep voice fell like a benediction.

'Welcome, daughter, to this rendezvous on the banks of the Green. Though it is a far cry from where last we met, it is a pleasure to see you again, Rowena.'

'Don Diego!' she gasped. 'What are *you* doing here—and in that garb, of all possible disguises!'

He did not offer to rise, but his smile held a hint of self-mockery.

'Disguise? You were ever apt of phrase, my dear. But does it not become me? I am more convinced each day that I have at last found my calling, my true avocation. Do I not make a seemly friar?'

103

Her lip curled. 'I seem to remember a couplet to the effect that when ill, the Devil a monk would be. But when well, the Devil a monk was he.'

'Excellent, my daughter! But surely you would not liken me to such as that?'

'You may wear the robes of a friar, Don Diego d'Ogeron, but it would take more than clothes to make a holy man of you. I've no doubt you stole them.'

'Not quite,' he denied, and the mocking twist was still at his lips. 'Your mood is something sharp, but that is understandable and so forgivable. As for these garments I wear, they might be called a gift. The good brother of St. Benedict who once wore them—I believe that was his order—was so kindly of spirit as to try to assist me. It was an ill-advised moment, with the sad result that he stopped an arrow intended for my own unwilling flesh. Apaches, you see, had flushed me like a quail.' Don Diego's sigh was heartfelt.

'I was filled with regret, but it would have been less than grateful to allow his sacrifice to be wasted. It had been an error, his receiving the arrow, for I find that a great many of our noble red brothers hold the black robes in more reverence than ever I had suspected. So I divested myself of my own poor garments and put them upon him—in short, I made a trade, before the Apaches discovered their mistake. Thanks to it, I am still alive to breathe the good clean air.'

'Say, rather, to pollute it!'

'I find you of an even greater spleen than in the old days. You should strive to control your temper, my daughter.'

'The role of a clergyman hardly becomes you!'

'Indeed? I had hoped that I was doing a passable job. But it is surprising—as surprising as pleasant to find you here, Rowena. I had supposed that you would be at least as far away as your native town.'

'Finding you here is no less of a surprise, but that is as far as I can go!'

His smile was a curious mixture of mockery and gentleness.

'I had hoped that you might like me better in this guise. Almost I had believed that some of the sanctity of these garments was rubbing off on me.'

'That, I never could believe!' Despite her curiosity, Rowena turned her back and hurried away. Of all the disquieting events of the day, finding Don Diego in this camp was the most upsetting.

It had made no whit of difference to the elegant Don Diego, at least outwardly, that his own government regarded him as a scoundrel of unmatched degree. It was whispered that some of his adventures as a soldier of fortune had been on the thin border of treason, and that the Spanish authorities would cheerfully hang him if they could lay hands upon him.

In other capitals he was tolerated. They had met in Paris, and almost from the start, Don Diego had fallen violently in love with the lady from Boston. Thereafter he had pursued Rowena with a fervor which she found frightening. Chiefly on his account, she had returned from Europe far ahead of her original plan.

And now he turned up here, at this far outpost! For the elegant Don, it was a setting as incongruous as the attire in which he masqueraded. She had no doubt that he had left Europe for reasons similar to those which had driven him from his native land. In the disguise of a priest he was certainly no more to be trusted than before.

She hesitated at the log, wondering how she had crossed it before, then set her teeth and managed. The waters of the river were swift and turbulent, and the accomplishment produced a small glow, quickly forgotten as she neared the tent. She still was in no mood to face Lexie.

For a while she followed up the bank of the stream, until she could hear voices from the camp. Both were very earnest, and one belonged to Don Diego.

It was disturbing that Paul should be friendly with such a man. But Don Diego had a charm of which she was well aware, and probably Higginson accepted him for what he seemed, a wearer of the cloth.

Rowena's excitement drained out, leaving her tired and uncertain. The arrival at the rendezvous was not at all as she had pictured it. She had half-hoped that something might occur to give a measure of justification to what she must do—but she had wanted nothing like this!

In that mood, she became aware of a change in the camp. There had been something of an air of holiday when she arrived. That was gone now. On either side of the water barrier, men gathered in little groups, voices raised angrily. Several mountain men clustered about a fire.

'I, for one, don't believe it!' The speaker's words were spaced and even, and despite nondescript garments his dignity matched that of an ambassador. 'I been with Irons many a time. We went through Blackfoot country together when they had a strong itchin' for our scalps. Boated down the Yellowstone in a bullhide. Froze on the Judith an' roasted on the Truckee. Pete's been there, same as us. He wouldn't do no such a trick.'

'It's told that he's workin' for Parks an' Burley. He brung the word.'

'Parks is a yappin' coyote. Him an' Burley don't run the same trail.'

'Burley used to be a trapper. So did Irons. But don't forgit, they both been to St. Louis. Burley's the Mountain. Now seems like Irons has throwed in with him. I tell you, a man turns buyer, it ain't the same.'

'Might be you got somethin' there.' Another man, silent till now, seemed to uncork speech by removing a stubby pipe. 'Plews I savvy, but money—a man gets it in his fist and it ain't never enough. The more he gets, the more he hankers after. Turns a man mean an' warped, seems like.'

'They's one way to tell.' A snow-headed trapper, still upright as a young sapling, spoke quietly, and the others listened attentively. 'Higginson's a fox, like his partner Parks. Fox an' half-skunk. Burley ain't never been that way, no more'n Pete Irons. Jim Hammond is Burley's buyer. We'll go make palaver. If they're all in together, we'll know it. If they ain't, we'll know that, too.'

'Irons has been with Hammond most of the time since he got here.'

'We'll see,' was the unruffled retort. 'Better to know where you stand 'fore you get riled.'

The group moved off, and Rowena followed at a discreet distance, unwillingly, yet impelled by a sense of foreboding. They would receive the same answer from Hammond—it could not be otherwise. When the bad news was confirmed—what then?

Why should they blame Irons? He was only a messenger. Yet already the word had spread and the onus was being flung at him. There was something sinister here. What had the trapper called Higginson? Half-fox, half-skunk. Such an opinion, in which the others had seemed tacitly to concur, was the judgment of men associated with him, and not to be lightly dismissed.

The trappers, now a dozen strong, came to a halt. Moving before them, crossing the log which spanned the Green and heading also for the trading headquarters, was another deputation, made up of Indians. Fully a score were in the group, half of them dressed in impressive feathered regalia which could only belong to chiefs or leading men. It did not require the word of the white-haired trapper to understand what was happening.

'The Injuns are scared too, an' sore. They're wantin' the low-down. We'll just stretch our ears a spell.'

'Dang me for a bobcat if I ever figgered to be on the same side with an Injun,' one trapper muttered. 'But mebby so we're all on two sides o' the same tree.'

A nervous clerk listened as one of the chiefs spoke. He had the look of a man of the cities, not yet sure of himself in this environment. He disappeared within the big tepee, then came back out. Irons and Hammond came also, the latter limping.

The Indians wasted no time in formality. That was right and proper on most occasions, and it was a measure of their unrest that they ignored it now.

'We go to Higginson,' the spokesman said. 'Want trade. Price about fixed. Now he tell us, not two beaver for one stick tobacco. *Four* beaver. Same all way. We like better two sticks tobacco, one skin.'

Irons and Hammond exchanged glances. The news had spread fast, and already it was taking an ugly turn.

'What else did Higginson tell you?' Hammond demanded.

'Say price in half. Say what Irons order.'

'That's a lie,' Irons retorted. 'I haven't talked to him or told him anything. He buys for himself, and can pay what he chooses.'

The chief grunted. There was a way to tell. Words were cheap—more so, often, than plews seemed now to be.

'You an' him not together?' he asked.

'I'm with Burley, and you all know the Mountain. They don't work with Parks and Higginson.'

'Then he lie, eh?' The chief's tone was oily now. 'The Mountain, you pay same price, like before? Two beaver, one stick tobacco?'

Hammond's oblique glance was full of question. Irons' mouth felt as bitter as when he'd had lung fever on the banks of the Judith, and his gaze, roving beyond the

Indians, saw the gathered trappers; he picked out Rowena in the background and saw her start guiltily. It was not enough that she had used him, making him a dupe, while she had come here to marry Higginson; she had sucked him dry along the way, casting him aside now like a skinned carcass.

Knowing that she was aligned with Higginson, it was only to be expected that she should tell all. Why stoop to half-treachery, or slice betrayal thin? But such thoughts puckered his mouth like green chokecherries.

This was a showdown. Now was the chance to speak, to prove Higginson a man of forked tongue and so ruin him forever. The trouble was that in the process he would as surely ruin Peter Burley. But by confirming Higginson's words, he would assume the guilt in all eyes, and bring a sort of triumph and vindication to his enemies.

CHAPTER NINE

'A winter pelt is good,' Irons said slowly, seeking for words which would bring understanding. 'The fur is long and thick, to warm a man. But the plew of a summer beaver is like bones which the dogs have gnawed. It is the same with men. When they are cold, they trade for skins with which to warm themselves. But when the sun warms them, they cast aside the skin.'

The chief grunted.

'But winter will come again,' he pointed out.

'It will come again,' Irons assented. 'But men change like the seasons. They who live far across the great water think new thoughts. They throw away the hides.'

The chief's arm swept in a wide gesture.

'This land is wide,' he said with dignity. 'But the snows come early, and the winds blow cold. We of the hills or of the plains work long; we toil while it is day and far into the night to trap the beaver.' He spoke in his native tongue, but many among both the trappers and the other tribes could understand. For those who could not, friends interpreted.

'We cannot rest when the blizzard howls,' he continued. 'Nor crouch close beside the fire. We must be out on the streams, for it is the rule of the trader that only if we bring many plews can we trade them for powder and for cloth. Without trade, in the time of the long cold, we perish.'

'That is true,' Irons acknowledged.

The chief's voice was triumphant.

'Are not all men the same when the cold descends upon the tepee? Must they not have skins to warm them, particularly if they have cast aside the old ones when the sun shone hot?'

That was unassailable logic, from their point of view, and Irons could think of no words to bridge the gap. To discuss bank policies, and hard times born of such fear, would merely engender fear of the Great White Father at Washington without removing a single stone in their path.

Nor could they ever comprehend white men and women who were the slaves to capricious fashion, particularly those arbiters of style who were above toil and want. Such a state of existence was simply unthinkable.

To the Indian, style changes for the sake of being different or up to date were unknown. Their way of life had been changed by the coming of the mountain men, the introduction of guns and traps and a chance to trade. But basically they had held to the pattern of past ages. Their tepees were made in the same design which the oldest squaw remembered, the style of clothing was planned for maximum utility. Adornment was secondary, never primary. It would be unthinkable to make an alteration for the sake of vanity.

Irons' silence was taken for consent. The chief pounced.

'Is there famine across the Great Water, that many die?' he asked. 'Or has a plague run like fire in grass across the land? Do only a handful huddle, shivering, in their tepees, where before the village was crowded? Is laughter stilled among the children? Do the warriors hunt in vain, the old men draw their robes about them and vanish into the night that the young may eat? Do the squaws crawl on hands and knees, digging for roots because there is no meat?'

'No,' Irons admitted. 'It is not like that.'

'Then, if there is no famine and no plague, when the cold returns again, they will need skins to warm them. Nothing is changed.'

The dark circle of faces remained impassive, but eyes glinted with triumph, and some of the listening trappers grunted approval. The chief had made what seemed to them an unassailable case.

The number of mountain men was increasing steadily. They came, silent and watchful, intent as on a hunt, for this was serious. The spirit of holiday, always attendant upon the rendezvous, had vanished. Among them Irons recognized men who had been his friends, but he saw only hostility or suspended judgment in their faces now. A voice from among them challenged.

'What you got to say to that? Still cuttin' the price in half, Trader? You hamstringin' us like a wolf does a moose?'

'Trader,' in such a tone of voice, was a slur, particularly when addressed to a mountain man. Irons' fists balled at his sides.

'The market in Europe is in bad shape,' he

114

said sharply. 'The fur houses there have quit buying. Pete Burley hopes there'll still be some market, and he knows you need to sell your plews. So he's still willing to buy. But if he was to pay the old price, and go broke, then when next summer comes there will be no buyers at all, nobody to trade at any price. Do you think I like this any better than he does? I'm a trapper, same as the rest of you.'

Even as he argued, he realized how useless it was to palaver. Men could talk when their ears were open, settling almost any sort of argument. But when they erected a wall of stubbornness or hate, words beat futilely on the air. In such a mood, men resorted to battle.

'You was a trapper,' was the stinging retort. 'Now you're cuttin' the price and cuttin' our throats. Is that it?'

'The price is cut,' Irons acknowledged, and blood pounded in his temples at the sly insult in the dissenter's voice. 'Who are you? Step out where I can see you.'

'I'll step out, all right.' The speaker pushed forward, swinging arms and shoulders to clear a way, and Irons felt his nerves crawl with recognition. This man he had last seen at the Platte—the wearer of the hob-nailed boots. Out of necessity, they had left him and his partners alive, when freeing the young Indian. That the trio should already have reached the rendezvous staggered him.

'Take a look,' Clubfoot mocked. 'Didn't expect to see me again, did you? Remember how you jumped me an' my pards, back at the Platte? You got the drop an' stole our winter's ketch, then set us afoot! You didn't figger we could live long 'thout guns or grub, but we made out to fool you. We're here. And as a trapper, I'm aimin' at a settlement! You been givin' us a lot o' guff! It's only you that's fixin' the price o' plews!'

'That's a lie!' Irons said flatly. Words had run out, and he welcomed something tangible at which he could hit back.

There had been a knife in Clubfoot's fist when Irons had first seen him, a blade thrown with deadly accuracy to thud into the logs of the old shack, grazing the skin of the captive Indian boy. There was the same knife in his hand now, the weapon with the red handle.

'A lie, is it? We'll see who's lyin'!' Having made his case, Clubfoot lunged ahead, in no way hampered by his disability. Murder should win sympathy rather than disapproval, under the circumstances, and he was sure of himself.

Irons twisted aside as the blade slashed, feeling the steel catch in the cloth at his shoulder and rip upward, the tip grazing his skin. A knife had never been his weapon, but the hampering cloth slowed the stroke, and Irons' fingers closed on Clubfoot's wrist.

For a long moment they faced each other,

arms corded with effort, scarcely moving. The renegade intended to kill. Once, Irons had had many friends among the onlookers, but their doubts had been stirred, and in any case a fight was rarely cause for interference. A mountain man defended himself. If he could not, he was no trapper, nor could he long expect to survive the other hazards of the land.

For seconds which took on the feel of hours they strained, wrist to wrist, muscles cording in arms and faces. But for the sweat which popped through the skin, the glitter of eyes, they might have been posturing. The white-headed trapper scrubbed palms on thighs in sweating excitement.

Twisting suddenly, Clubfoot brought up a knee in a quick thrust for the groin, and at the same instant his teeth snapped at Irons' nose. Such tactics had won more than one battle, but Irons was long schooled in trickery. He twisted aside without relaxing his grip on the knife-wrist, and his leg, thrust forward, locked under Clubfoot's lifted ankle.

Again they strained, refusing to fall. Panting lungs made a hoarse wheeze, and abruptly the effort was too great. The knife slipped from loosened fingers and fell, and Clubfoot wrenched backward, breaking free.

Irons had sensed the danger in him before they clashed. Most men on this border fought with the instinct of savagery, like animals.

Clubfoot was more like a falcon harrying, a kingfisher, planning the attack, a move ahead. Even as he lunged back out of reach, he twisted and reached for the knife. He snatched it, and his run took him out of reach.

He reversed, face twisting horribly with the mind's intent, arm drawn back and flung in a sweeping gesture, and the blade drove like a bullet. Irons sensed the trick and threw himself flat. The knife was a slash of silver between the circle of onlookers, and the whole line jerked back.

Face down, Irons thrust with his palms, turning to meet the expected attack. But rather than come to grips without his weapon, Clubfoot ran for it, foregoing the momentary advantage.

Holding the knife again, he advanced, and Irons backed, eyes on the glitter of the blade. Out of the corner of his eye he saw Hammond, his face flat with strain. Shawneen stood beside him. At the far apex of the crowd Higginson leaned forward, a dreadful expectancy in his eyes.

Clubfoot advanced in a half-crouch, his tongue playing across lips avid with the taste for blood. The circle became a broken U, opening to give them passage, closing raggedly behind. Close at hand sounded the muffled surge of the Green, raging at hampering banks.

Irons understood his opponent's purpose, to crowd him to the riverbank, hampering his movements. Coming to grips again with steel snake-quick in its dart was the alternative.

The riverbank fell away, a deceptive terminal. Winter snows, deep along the mountain watershed, had become changelings in unseemly haste during the last run of spring. The raw breath of chinook winds, tempered by the northward-plunging sun, had worked the seasonal miracle. Flood torrents had jostled for place in an overfull channel. Straining for room, the current had clawed the softened bank, ripping it loose in huge chunks.

A pine tree had been undermined and toppled. All that remained visible from above was an upthrust of tangled roots. Irons stumbled back, over the edge. Triumph swelled in Clubfoot's throat and burst forth like the gobble of a turkey. The sound ended in gasping alarm as he tried to draw back.

That he was taking a long chance, Irons knew. But only in a calculated risk could such odds be matched. As his feet churned at emptiness, he grabbed one of the holding roots and clung. His other hand clamped on Clubfoot before he could retreat. Now the odds were turned.

It was thirty feet down to the river. Not a long drop with water to break the fall, but height and water alike held terrors for

Clubfoot greater than the fear which his knife had inspired in Irons. No wild beast in a trap was more desperate. Irons shifted his other hand, letting go the root.

Only desperation enabled Clubfoot to pull back, teetering on the brink, with Irons' weight dragging at him. His frantic backward lunge overbalanced him, and he went down with Irons on top. The knife came loose, and Irons finally had possession.

He poised it above the cringing renegade, muscles taut with the will to thrust. For a moment, while lungs strained for air, he hesitated. The sensible way was to end this menace, driving the blade to its hilt, as Clubfoot would do if their positions were reversed. Not a man among the onlookers expected any other end.

Apparently he wasn't the man he once had been. Softness had come upon him like a plague from the town, though not the flabbiness he'd feared that blustery spring day. He was as rock-hard and sinewy as ever. Maybe the softness had developed along the trail, when a woman rode beside him. When a man gave way to dreams, he was either very young or very old.

Savagely he came to his feet, and the cringing man on the ground could not know that his rage rooted in self-scorn. Words snarled from clenched teeth.

'Get out!' Irons rasped. 'Next time, I'll kill

you!'

Clubfoot scuttled away. Irons' glance raked the crowd, then came back to his hand. He still held the knife, its red-painted handle like blood between his fingers.

For a moment he eyed it between wonder and disgust. The blade was overlong, and around the edges of the steel and the joining of the handle showed an old stain, turned dingy brown.

His face blank and tight, Irons strode away. Halfway back to his own quarters, remembering the knife, he hurled it toward the Green.

*　　*　　*

The fight had put a period to questions. Neither red men nor white, after witnessing the struggle, had any remaining doubts. Whatever might be said for or against him, Irons was still of the mountain men. The word which he brought was law.

Now his edict was beyond dispute. The price of beaver was cut in half.

Irons noted, with wry amusement, that few of the trappers sought him out with congratulations or in a renewal of friendship. Your mountain man became a creature of his environment. The wild entered into him. As he grew alien to the life he once had known, so did its ways become strange to him. Like a coyote, he traveled for the most part alone, with only a limited trust in anyone but himself. Even friendship was a guarded thing, like the present truce with the Indians. A matter of miles or hours could make a difference wide as life and death.

To accept the verdict was one thing. To approve it was something else, and nothing could compel them to that, or to liking for the man who carried enforcement in iron fists. In their minds the blame was fixed on him.

The loneliness ate at him like acid. Never before had he felt out of place in this land. He had often been lonesome in St. Louis, particularly when men moved on every side with no thought beyond their own concerns, but that was different. To feel so here was to find himself alien indeed, a wanderer cast forth from Eden. He tramped most of the night away, his thoughts less on Clubfoot, who might stalk him treacherously, or on the problem of beaver, than on Rowena. If she was faithless, the world was indeed a lonely place. And what else was there to believe?

Higginson watched while the fight continued, such eagerness in him that he could scarcely control himself. Craftily he had worked that afternoon to fasten the onus of the cut price upon Irons.

He was aware that his dislike for the man was rooted in the primitive, stemming from jealousy. Rowena had come a long way under the protection of Irons, and in his company. Her very lack of words had given him a bitter insight into her liking for the man. She had betrayed Irons to him, because she had pledged herself to him. But despite the hurt in her, from what she had seen between Irons and Running Fawn, Higginson could see a deeper flowing current, more powerful even than she guessed.

Exultation squeezed out of his bloodstream, and fear took its place as Clubfoot was vanquished. Bitterness could scarcely be stronger in the renegade than the raw taste of the bile in his own throat. As Clubfoot slunk away, Higginson also moved like a creature of the darkness. Gripped by this far from amiable mood, he put aside the flap of his tepee, then stopped in a black rage.

Running Fawn was waiting for him, once again cross-legged on the pile of buffalo robes, a slender, seductive figure in the dusk. His mirror was propped on her rounded knees, and she peered into it, working to redden already scarlet lips with the boiled blood-red of a root.

She was striving to make herself desirable in his eyes, practicing the tricks of her vainer sisters, and such of those of the white women as experience had taught. Once the exhibition would have amused him, but now it frightened. Here was more trouble, and Higginson shrank from an ordeal he'd temporarily put out of mind.

'You should be at your father's tepee,' he said harshly. 'Not here.'

'Why not here?' Running Fawn countered. 'Did you not purchase me, for your own tepee? I no longer belong in my father's.'

'I told you that I must have a few days in which to work,' he protested. 'Don't you understand?'

'Could I fail to do so? You want days in which to make love to the white woman! Time to marry her!'

'I didn't expect her to come here,' Higginson argued wearily. 'This has taken me by surprise—'

'But it had been arranged that she should come,' Running Fawn reminded him. 'Do you but play with all women? I thought that white men were faithless only to squaws! Does no one mean anything to you?'

Higginson winced. This untutored savage had a way of getting under his skin, and no compunction about doing so.

'I tell you it's a mistake,' he growled. 'You did a good job this afternoon,' he added hoping to placate her. 'That sure took Irons by surprise.'

'That was a mistake, that I should do it,' Running Fawn said calmly. 'I played your game, and you used it to trick me into silence. In return for serving you, now you would cast me off.'

'You know better than that. It's only for a few days—'

'A few? How many days make a moon? How many moons before the sun grows cold and Running Fawn, cast off, would shiver in her tepee, while the other squaws laugh in scorn? Are those days only while Rendezvous lasts? That I could endure, but I read your heart, and it is cold. Again you would lie to me, for when this is over, she will return to her land, and you will go with her. My heart is to be left like an empty campground.'

Lithely she sprang to her feet, confronting him. Eyes flashing, she was all savage, yet all the woman. The pent-up storm broke.

'Do you think that I will be cast aside like a broken arrow? You tell me to return to the tepee of my father. Shall I go there like a dog kicked from yours? Rather will I die!'

Higginson tried to argue, to explain. With nerves already ragged, panic seized him as she remained adamant. Someone might come at any moment, quite possibly Rowena. This had to be settled, resolved in some manner, and finally. He must be rid of Running Fawn, since she was in a mood to cause trouble. If Rowena ever learned the truth, he would lose her, for she could be as fiercely proud as this Pawnee woman. It was that quality which had first attracted him in each. Both were of the pioneers.

His mind leaped ahead, and there was only

disaster along the trail. Rowena, if she learned of his treachery, would go to Irons. If she did not yet understand how he had turned the anger of the trappers against Irons, she must soon learn. With her word to back Irons, and hated as Higginson knew himself to be, the revulsion of feeling would be explosive.

His panic became a red haze. Running Fawn's voice was rising, half in anger, but partly with deliberate intent that they should be overheard. Higginson caught at her, his fingers closing on her throat. Her taunting smile crazed him as it clung to her scarlet mouth.

Running Fawn struggled, lithe and strong with the heritage of her race. But he was powerful, and rage increased his strength. Only when Running Fawn sagged, a limp weight in his arms, did reason break through the scarlet fog.

He released her, his hands falling, and she slumped at his feet. Higginson stared down at the suddenly inert form, which only moments before had been vibrant with life. A fresh surge of fear swept him, cold where its forerunner had scorched. He dropped to his knees, calling her name, snatching her up against himself, observing how loosely her head rolled on her shoulders.

A scream choked in his throat as he made sure that she was dead. A moment longer he clutched her, holding her to him as if to give back from himself life. Her warmth was still strong and vital, and in a revulsion of feeling he buried his face in her breast. Too late, the truth came to him, numbing as it was revealing. He loved her. She was the only woman he had ever loved, and he had killed her.

The sound of approaching footsteps brought him, wild and disheveled, to his feet.

There wasn't much time. He grabbed Running Fawn by the arm and tugged her back, covering her with the pile of buffalo robes. When it was done they looked crumpled, but much as usual. With an effort he steadied the rasp of breath in his throat and schooled his face as Yosemite called, then thrust aside the flap.

'What the devil do you want?' Higginson demanded, and the trapper shrank from the glare in his eyes.

'Why—why, nothin' much, Mr. Higginson,' he protested, but his eyes were bold and questing as those of a fox. 'On'y—why, Frenchy wanted me to find out what we're going to do about the tradin'—'

With an effort, Higginson brought his mind back to such problems, which were pressing. He stepped outside, forcing Yosemite ahead, and again he was able to think in accustomed grooves.

'I suppose we'll buy what's offered, at the

cut price,' he said. 'We ought to get the big share of what's to be had, considerin'.'

'Yeah. Mebby. That all you got in mind?' Yosemite sounded disappointed. 'Frenchy, he figgered you'd have a scheme. Most everybody's pretty mad at the Mountain— and I thought we'd cash in.'

It took a physical effort to turn his face away from the tepee, but Higginson managed. He stroked his chin with uncertain fingers.

'You're right,' he agreed. 'I have been doing some thinking—I was sittin' there alone, figuring, and that's why I hated to be disturbed. But I believe I know how to work it. Listen!'

He gave orders, low-voiced, the words tumbling over one another as the scheme took shape and his thoughts outraced his tongue. After Yosemite had departed to begin their execution, Higginson stared after him, and only another look back at the dreadfully silent tepee shook his complacency.

Ordinarily a squaw was a squaw, the property of the man who bought her. He could do pretty much as he pleased, and no questions asked. But in this case, Running Fawn had been a chief's daughter. That, with all the complicating factors, made an ugly situation.

Slowly he turned. The Green flowed wide and shallow at the spot where Irons had flung

128

away the knife. Maybe—

An hour later, his quest rewarded, Higginson was turning homeward when he saw another man, moving with a weary stride which still held an element of restlessness. With sharpened perceptions, he recognized Irons.

So you're having a bad time of it, too, he thought. Enjoy yourself, for it'll be worse!

A trapper, rolled in half an ancient buffalo hide beside the ashes of a fire, stirred with disconcerting quickness. He half-reached for his rifle, then relaxed as he recognized the trader.

'What the blazes you doin', prowlin' at this hour?' he demanded. 'Don't you ever sleep, boss?'

'I've been asleep,' Higginson said glibly. 'Then Frenchy woke me with some questions about the tradin'. I'm not the only one,' he added, and pointed to the dimming figure. 'There's Irons. Where you reckon he's been?' He forced a chuckle which rasped his mouth.

'I could make a guess at that,' he added. 'After the way that Pawnee gal ran to him, the minute he showed up in camp! Yeah, this plew-puller could sure make a guess!'

CHAPTER TEN

The sun shone bright across the valley of the Green. But today it would take more than the sun to dispel the gloom that had settled like fog at his coming. Irons sensed an air of sullenness as he looked over the camp, slower than usual in stirring to activity. Today, trading should get under way. All the usual preliminaries had been disposed of, the haggling and the feeling-out. Men were growing impatient to drink strong whiskey or to own new guns. Squaws who had accompanied their men craved bright cloth and fancy trinkets. A season's take was to be spent.

Even at a cut price, trading must proceed. But a night of pondering, followed by sunshine, could not push aside the evil news like a bad dream. Half a season's toil was the same as wasted. The skilled or the lucky, who yesterday had accounted themselves rich, awoke poor. The unlucky and the lazy faced destitution.

Irons had known how it must be, pondering the problem in the long weeks and miles of the trail, hating his own part. But this was a harsh land, as reality usually was. Here, only the strong survived. It was nature's way, and perhaps it was best. But

130

those who were trampled could not be expected to kiss the feet which spurned them.

It had been a bad night. The realities of the situation were not enough to keep his mind from Rowena. She had misunderstood, of course, when that Indian girl had greeted him like a returning lover. That might account, in part, for what she had done. It could not excuse all, and his mind turned back upon itself like a treadmill.

To his surprise, trade began early at the headquarters set up by the Mountain, and grew brisk as the day wore on. Hammond, Irons, and a couple of clerks were kept busy. Irons welcomed the work; it kept him occupied, and it seemed to promise an acceptance of the situation. Indians and mountain men were coming, about equally.

Shawneen glowered suspiciously at such a ready acceptance of the change. Growling, he stalked away, returning in a mood even more dour.

'Seems like we're doin' five times as much business as Higginson,' he reported. 'Which ain't in natur'. Makes this ol' mule as leery as the smell of a rattler.'

'We're here to buy fur,' Irons reminded him. 'Without plews the Mountain would go out of business.'

'Might be the same this way, only quicker,' Shawneen grunted, and continued on his rounds. By noon he was back again.

'There's a smell o' skunk in the wind,' he said bluntly. 'For one thing, there's a gob o' bad whiskey bein' swallered. Everywhere you go, men are guzzlin'. And that's a matter o' wonder, for *we're* doin' the tradin'—and it ain't in whiskey.'

There could be only one source for the liquor. Shawneen waved a gnarled thumb.

'Higginson's clerks are passin' it out, an' he's drinkin' his full share o' the p'izen. Likewise, he's doin' a power o' talkin' with the trappers. Red or white, seems all the same. He's friendly with them as powder to a gun. They palaver a spell with him, drink his whiskey, *then* come *here* to trade!'

Shawneen was not alone in his unease. Rowena was prey to increasing apprehension as the day wore on. She walked, this morning, arm in arm with Lexie, wishing almost that her aunt would chide her for her conduct. Lexie's complete forbearance, her gentle understanding, both helped and hurt.

She had expected that Higginson would spend the previous evening visiting with them, but had found excuses for his absence. But she had been sure that he would be ready to give much of his time to her today, and the fact that he had looked in for only a brief greeting at breakfast was disturbing. Reports of Irons' epic battle of the evening had reached them, along with the identity of his opponent.

'It was that dreadful clubfooted man.' Rowena shuddered. 'He tried to murder him! He should have been killed when we found him first! If it hadn't been for us, he would.'

Lexie did not seem bewildered by her niece's reckless misuse of pronouns, or in doubt as to her meaning.

'It's too bad he didn't,' she agreed.

'I suppose I'd have been horrified—then!' Rowena added. 'Now I wish they had!'

'I'm afraid we've both made a lot of mistakes, on this journey,' Lexie said soberly.

Rowena eyed her sharply, then her eyes filled, and she blinked rapidly.

'I know *I* have,' she conceded. 'I—But what's the use! Lexie, look at those canoes! I wonder if we could borrow or rent one? I've got to do *something*,' she added, 'or I'll go crazy.'

Both of them were proficient with a boat or canoe, and three of the latter were drawn up on the bank, above a gentle pool. Rowena approached a trapper who idled in the sun, back to a tree, and explained what they had in mind.

'If you could tell us how to find the owner of the canoe,' she added, and paused uncertainly.

The trapper, head turned studiously away, listened in silence, then shook his head.

'Why now, 'twouldn't be too hard,' he sighed. 'Them's Injun craft, and I reckon

133

they could be borreyed. But you wouldn't want to, nohow.'

'Why not?' Rowena challenged.

'Why now, the main reason is, the Green, hereabouts, ain't no place for fun.' He faced them momentarily, and Rowena blanched at a whiff of his breath. 'The old crick, she gets mean an' cantankerous as a bear with a sore paw right sudden.'

Seeing the look on her face, he hastily turned his back again, then sauntered away, trying desperately to make both feet track together. There seemed no more to be said, and Rowena accepted the verdict. But her eyes were bright.

'Lexie!' she exclaimed. 'He was drunk! This early in the day!'

'There seems to be a lot of drinking going on,' Lexie admitted. 'You can see it everywhere.'

'I'm going to find Paul and speak to him. It's disgraceful.'

'Maybe that's one more matter we should accept as we find it,' Lexie suggested.

But Rowena was adamant. They found Higginson, and Rowena lost no time in stating her views.

'Yeah, this whiskey drinkin' is bad,' Higginson conceded. 'But the Mountain's getting all the business today, doing all the trading. Draw your own conclusions!'

He excused himself and hurried away.

Rowena looked after him with narrowed eyes.

'Now, that's funny!' she said.

'You mean that he's half-drunk himself?'

'I noticed that, but it's not what I meant. Why should the Mountain be getting all the business? Everybody seems to be friendly with Paul, and they're all mad at—at Peter Irons! So you'd think it would be just the other way around!'

Lexie shook her head, perplexed.

'And Paul wasn't a bit displeased,' she added shrewdly. 'I don't understand, but I'm afraid that we're only babes in the wood, out here. I think we'd better go back to our tent.'

Later in the day, Higginson came by, and Rowena viewed him with dismay. If he had been half-drunk at midmorning, he was completely under the influence now. Not that it affected him as it did many. He could carry his liquor with scarcely a slurring of words or uncertainty in gait. With him it showed in other ways. Why he should drink so heavily Rowena could not understand, knowing nothing of the remorse and terror which he sought desperately to drown. In that purpose he had succeeded, reaching a point of boastful arrogance.

'I reckon Irons thinks he's smart!' he said, and at mention of his rival's name his eyes were red with more than liquor. 'Getting all the fur! Hah! If he only knew!'

'What do you mean?' Rowena demanded,

and her suspicions sharpened.

'He'll find out!' Higginson prophesied darkly. 'Smart, eh? We'll see who takes the plews out! See who's clever! You bet.'

Brusquely refusing to linger, he strode away. The two women exchanged glances, then cast a look about the big camp. The sun was close to setting, and the trappers were becoming boisterous as the day waned. Rowena shivered involuntarily, then frowned as a black-robed figure came toward them.

A glance assured her of Don Diego's sobriety. He could carry his liquor well, but in this debauchery, he seemed an example of probity. His bow was grave, belied by the half-amused mockery in his eyes—self-mockery, as his words confirmed.

'I come to you ladies as your father confessor,' he murmured. 'For once, these robes do more than swaddle me in heat. But if you don't care for me in that role, might I come as a friend—a friend of other days?'

'Is not one role as false as the other?' Rowena challenged, and again he bowed with mock humility.

'Perhaps you are right.' His eyes ranged the camp, and levity was replaced by gravity.

'I am well aware of your opinion of me, Rowena. And I admit it to be deserved. But please credit me with one instance of sincerity in a misspent life. At a time like this, I could not be true to—to these garments in which I posture if I stayed away. I wanted to make sure that you understood the situation.' Again his glance raked the camp, disgust pinching his aristocratic face. 'I have been in unpromising situations before, but nothing such as this. It is my hope that you ladies will stay together, and in your own tent.'

It was Lexie who answered.

'Thank you,' she agreed. 'That seems like good advice.'

'I can think of none better, except that you should have friends, or should I say guards, near at hand,' Don Diego murmured. 'I supposed that Mr. Higginson would have taken precautions to insure your safety, but I see none. If you ask why, having both eyes and ears, I can only say that a devil's brew has been cooking all day. In the forceful parlance of the mountain men, hell is due to bust loose. And tonight I dislike the dark.'

Rowena shivered. It would be a drunken, riotous night, from all the portents. If only Peter Irons were beside the fire, as he had been on the trail! But he was no longer looking after their welfare, nor could he be expected to. That was Higginson's task, and apparently he was too drunk to be concerned.

The sun had set and dusk was closing over the valley. Voices came louder than before, and in them could be sensed what Diego had implied—that drunken men would be as wild as their nature, holding high revel before falling soddenly asleep.

A cry rang out, cutting short the clamor, stilling the camp. The awful, keening death wail of the Indian.

The sound arrested the rising clamor like a rock thrown into a pool. But where the stone would set ripples spreading, the high-pitched note seemed rather to draw them back, as though concentrating fear. It was a cry of loneliness and terror, of grief at a soul's ascending.

Irons heard the shout and stiffened, his mind, tired from the long day following a weary night, instantly classifying. That was a live Indian raising his wail at sight of the dead. A dead Indian, for only one of their own blood would merit the call.

Indians differed widely as to tribe and custom, but in that one point they were alike. And in such a matter nearly all of them would feel alike. What was worse, they might act in concert.

The trend of the day, the heavy trading, centering at their outpost, along with Shawneen's forebodings, had not been lost upon Irons. But this situation was like scaling the face of a cliff. To go higher might mean disaster, but to turn back was impossible.

All noise ended, then took up again, but on a new note, rife with apprehension. In the camp of the mountain men, trappers had been singing or yelling, drunken ribaldry in which ugliness overshadowed exuberance. Across the Green, the noise was in a different tempo, but everywhere it was bad liquor speaking. Irons had seen such conditions before, but on a smaller scale. Never had there been a gathering like this, the mass intoxicated with liquor and hate. It was a bad mixture.

Shawneen came like a shadow. He was a man who liked his whiskey, and today it had been everywhere, but he was cold sober. His fingers gripped white about his rifle.

'That makes two,' he said. 'An Injun found another—you heard that yip!'

'Nothing wrong with my ears,' Irons conceded.

'It was a woman—a young squaw,' Shawneen went on. 'With a knife stickin' between her shoulder blades! She's the Injun who pawed you when we hit camp yesterday. This ain't purty.'

Summer heat had been oppressive during the afternoon, but Irons grew cold at the words. All day he'd felt what Don Diego had put into speech—that a devil's brew was being concocted.

'Dead,' Shawneen repeated. 'By a knife. An' she'd tangled with you! Makes for mean talk.'

'You mean that tongues are wagging?'

'If they wa'n't, they are. I wa'n't allowed to get close—but I found some out. This

139

Runnin' Fawn was stone cold, stiff. She'd been dead quite a spell. Which likely means she was kilt last night. Folks have been wonderin' about her. I heard some powwowin' doorin' the afternoon as to where she could have disappeared to.'

'What else?' Irons asked.

'Dunno. The Injuns are talkin' it over like one big fam'ly. Makin' medicine.'

He made as if to say more, peered closely at Irons' face, and swung away with the words unspoken. The old hoss was taking this hard. Anybody short of a fool could see, all the way from St. Louis, how he felt, and Shawneen wasn't blind when it came to reading sign. He'd been agin' it all from the start. Wimmin on the trail—

Even he'd been a softheaded fool, before they reached the hills. That pair had won him over, when he should have knowed better. But he'd somehow come to count on them. No wonder Irons was cut deeper than knife could slash—

Always it kept coming back to knives! A blade was an ugly weapon, and this purty leetle squaw—

Hours can run like a racing horse or walk with tired feet. This night was long. The wildly riotous course which it might have taken had been checked by the discovery of Running Fawn, and men's thoughts, particularly the long and devious ponderings

140

of the red men, turned into new channels.

Some among the braves were for immediate action and reprisal, but cooler judgment prevailed. A new chief, scarcely heard of until now, had risen to prominence. Big Eagle, of the Pawnees, was holding them in check. Since it was his daughter who lay dead, they listened with respect.

Shawneen, venturing as close as prudence dictated, made sure of this. He gave grudging respect to a bereft father who curbed his own passions at such a time, but he was not deceived.

'They're cookin' a pot of trouble for somebody,' he informed Irons. 'They're mad as a nest of hornets, but they're makin' mighty sure what they want before they start. Mebby it's good—but I suspicion it's like p'izen simmerin'. That's all any o' the whites know—yet!'

Celebration had halted abruptly on both sides of the river. No man was too drunk to misunderstand. Resentments of the past couple of days, piled atop old wrongs, could lead to anything. This was no time for revelry.

Rowena, at Lexie's insistence, finally agreed to rest. She was sure she could not sleep, but exhaustion took its toll.

Irons waited out the night. Ordinarily it would have held no mystery, but this was no common situation. To those who knew

Indians, and most of the mountain men had been well schooled, there was only one certainty—trouble. That sureness should have brought with it the conviction that the trappers would stand together; but nothing about this was normal or to be depended upon.

It was long after midnight when the powwow ended. Shadowy figures, made monstrous in reflected light, had squatted before leaping flames or stood to harangue, but sentinels posted had kept the overcurious among the trappers at a distance, and no one pressed too hard. It was better to wait, so long as there was deliberation. Only fools spilled the kettle of trouble.

Birds were beginning to chirp in restless anticipation of the dawn when a score of Indians came across the log in sober ambassadorship. Big Eagle stalked at their head.

Despite the hour, they found the white section of the camp awake, and that occasioned no surprise. This time they observed the formalities. In careful ceremonial, and the repression of emotion, lay a threat greater than the shaking tail of a rattlesnake.

Big Eagle made a speech. He might have been talking of someone far removed from his own family, as he pointed out that red men and white alike were gathered for the rendezvous, come here to trade in amity. The red men, like their white brothers, had toiled and endured hardship to secure a big catch of beaver. All had journeyed far.

It was leading up, like a slow stalking of game. White men, seeking to catch a wild horse, would pursue on others, a swift and desperate chase, won or lost in the first miles or minutes. Indians, even if lacking other horses with which to pursue, would trail the wild bunch on foot, a dogged perseverance enduring for days or weeks. In the end they would capture and tame the wildest of the bunch, and in such methods they had learned patience.

Big Eagle outlined the opening of the rendezvous, the arrival of the trappers and the coming of the traders, the preliminary bartering. All had been going normally and well until the arrival of the men from St. Louis.

Shawneen, crouched beside Irons, growled in his throat.

'This is like dippin' in the pot with one hand and holdin' yore nose with the other,' he grunted. 'He ain't bringin' *that* up for nothin'!'

The message which Irons had brought had changed everything. But that was bad news which affected every trapper equally, whether mountain men or Indian. Those tidings were ill, a drift of smoke on the wind, the odor of decaying dead above a deserted tepee in the first thaw of spring. Listening, while the chief talked, men stirred and nodded, without distinction as to color of skin.

There was mystery here, a hidden trail buried beneath snows too deep for even a skilled tracker to unravel. It lay not alone in the break in price. Many had witnessed the arrival of the trader, and had seen the sudden joy with which Running Fawn had rushed to greet a man who returned in the guise of a mountain man but who had proved to be no longer a trapper. If it was true that he had once drunk of the waters of Manitou, surely those waters had turned bitter in his belly.

Irons sat quietly aware that Shawneen, ever restless, had stolen away. What was the old chief driving at? There could no longer be any doubt that he was the target.

No man, the chief went on, who had watched or listened could doubt that Running Fawn had been eager. Love had shone from her eyes; it had sung in her greeting. But in return she had received hate. Irons had journeyed from a far country with another woman, and the welcoming words of Running Fawn had been an unwilling sound in his ears.

Big Eagle held his audience in his hand. Secure in that knowledge, he did not hurry. It had distressed his heart, as the father of Running Fawn, that his daughter should be so cast aside, but often that was the way with men. Craftily, he did not suggest that it was mostly the way of the mountain men, for no one could doubt that he sought to have all men on his side. Since it was also the way of men not to interfere in such affairs unless compelled, he, like Running Fawn, had suffered the hurt in silence.

But that was only a beginning. The real purpose of Irons' coming had quickly become known—an order to cut in half the price to be paid the trappers, all trappers. How bitterly that would affect each one, regardless of whether they were Indians or mountain men, he sketched in sonorous phrases. Like most of his kind, Big Eagle was an orator.

Abruptly he threw a question at them. Was the heart of this man good? If it were true, as he claimed, that men who dwelt far across the great water had tired of the wearing of skins and took no thought for the cold of winter, then there was cause for what he did. But if there had been no famine to decimate the population, all men knew that when the cold came again skins would be needed as they had been since the time of the Old Men. Always, after summer, came winter.

Was the heart of this man evil? Another white man had challenged him, and his charges had been grave. He had battled, but the medicine of Irons had proved stronger. Many had witnessed that fight. They had seen

Irons prevail, clutching in his hand the knife which he had wrested from his foe.

Cleverly, he made no further mention of the defeated man. That was in every mind, working like yeast.

The chief's voice dropped. His heart had been heavy with grief for his daughter, Running Fawn. She had been a comfort to him, like sunshine on a winter day. But when she had grown to womanhood and tasted the bitter, when he would have comforted her, she had not returned to his tepee.

No one could tell him of his daughter, who had not walked abroad in the camp. Fear had fastened its claws in his heart. Then, in the night, a Crow, hurrying to his own tepee, had stumbled across something in the path. His wail for the dead had proclaimed that he had found the body of Running Fawn.

Big Eagle's hand flashed upward, holding the knife with the red handle.

'Look upon this knife!' he trumpeted. 'This is the drinker of blood from her heart! Look, and then tell me if we have done right in coming to demand justice!'

CHAPTER ELEVEN

Irons, his back against a tree, had listened impassively, his arms folded. From the start it had been easy to see where the chief was leading, picking on him as a natural scapegoat. But even in their present mood of hostility, the trappers remained mountain men. They would require more than oratory to be convinced.

He took a quick step forward, then checked at sight of the knife. The thing was impossible, but there it was.

He had flung the knife into the river. At least, he'd hurled it toward the Green. But it must have fallen either on the sand or in shallow water, and someone had retrieved it.

Big Eagle had been impressive in building up his case. Now he was terrible in accusation.

'We have not leaped like a startled deer at a strange sound, to run wildly and perhaps foolishly,' he emphasized. 'Rather have we sat in the doors of our tepees, considering soberly, making sure. Only after we had pondered well did we come to you, and now we bring our evidence.'

His glance darted like a hummingbird, picking out faces which showed taut and strained in the fast-growing light.

'It was not easy to wait as does the vixen for the return of her mate, bringing meat for their young. A father's heart is like that vixen when the old fox fails to return.

'Now Running Fawn, like the young foxes, will play no more in the sun. Gone is the laughter from her lips, as her shadow from the campground. But behind her she leaves many friends who clamor for vengeance, even as the vixen growls in her throat.'

Irons listened with the rest. There could be no doubt of the chief's earnestness or sincerity. Now I know how a trapped beaver feels! Irons thought, while the words ran on.

'There is a sorrowing mother waiting on the banks of a distant stream. How shall I tell her that her daughter comes no more? The thoughts of the heart are like flame in dry grass. Some of our young braves feel with their hearts and, having more of valor than discretion, are at times unable to see clearly, to distinguish friend from foe.'

He was speaking in his own tongue, but everyone knew his theme. Those who failed to understand could guess.

Irons' gaze, like that of the others, remained on the red-handled knife which the chief still held aloft. It was the accuser, the more potent because it was mute.

'We are friends of the white men,' Big Eagle continued gravely. 'In a distant lodge, where the rivers run to meet the sun, we smoked the peace pipe, and our hearts were good. We have come to this meeting-place to trade in amity, and we would not have the occasion spoiled by strife. Our rules are simple: He who will not hunt shall not eat. He who does evil in the sight of the Great

Spirit shall have evil returned upon him. Those were our laws before the white man first saw the sun upon our mountains. They will be our laws when the sun last sets in the valleys.

'When the heart of a red man grows evil, we punish him as he deserves.' Slowly the glittering knife described an arc. 'So, we know, do you of the mountains deal with one of your own kind when into him goes the blood of a wolf.'

Both arms were outstretched, with the knife held between.

'Since a common wrong has been done all of us, this should not be a knife to sever, but a bond to unite us. This, we who share responsibility have pointed out to those overeager ones, constraining them to patience. Such patience as the vixen practices when the scent of the lynx grows faint in her nostrils! We have counseled patience that justice might be sure. But blood cries out for vengeance!'

With the first shock of surprise past, Irons watched, feeling remote and somehow detached. It was as though this did not concern him. He knew what was coming. Big Eagle made the demand simply, but it was that, rather than a request. They wanted only that the guilty should be punished, that the ancient laws be enforced. Turn Irons over to them, and they would make sure that he paid the penalty.

The chief left no doubt that their demand must be met. It was simple justice. If the mountain men were blind to fairness, mistakenly loyal to a man whose hands were red with murder; if they preferred to condone such conduct and protect him in infamy, then the reponsibility would rest upon them. In such a case, neither the young braves nor the older warriors could be restrained.

That, too, was simple truth. Not a mountain man worthy of the name but knew that Big Eagle had done a remarkable job in holding a drunken, angry host in check through the long night, keeping them tight-reined until they sobered. But for his fairness, there might easily have been a slaughter, red against white, with the odds overwhelmingly in favor of the Indians.

No right-minded man could blame them now. They were asking a minimum price, instead of giving way to a fury of vengeance such as might have been expected.

That put it up to him, and Irons knew what his decision must be. He felt no emotion. That had been drained from him when Rowena had gone to the arms of Higginson. His eyes ranged the taut faces of the other whites, and though they were devoid of expression, he knew what they were thinking.

Once there would have been no question about the mountain men standing by one of their own, whatever the cost. But in the eyes of most of them he was no longer a true mountain man. He had gone to the city, turning his back upon the hills. When he had returned it was almost in the guise of an enemy. He was alien, the waters of Manitou turned bitter in his belly, as the chief had said.

Many of them would fight for him, if he asked them to, because they had been his friends. If he called for a showdown, they were mountain men, a race apart and beyond the ordinary, like a white buffalo among the brown horde.

Even hating him, believing him guilty, they'd fight for him if he asked it. That was their code. But he would violate it in the asking. They looked at him and waited for what he had to say.

He could not prove his innocence, and that was what counted. The red-handled knife had last been seen in his hand, until it was found buried to its hilt in the soft flesh of Running Fawn. She had denounced him, but had apparently gone to a midnight tryst with him—and her death. He had been seen returning—and he had no witnesses that he had walked alone far up the Green.

The fury of the red men had been held in check through the night, but waters so pent increased in violence. If their temper was vented upon him, the rest of the camp would go free. But if he was denied them now, then that anger would be unleashed upon everyone. And particularly upon Rowena and Lexie, because they, by a complex chain, were linked with him and with the death of Running Fawn.

Because of them, he had killed her. If trouble started—Irons shook his head. He couldn't let it.

He moved out from the tree, feeling the weight of sleepless hours upon him, knowing how slow this day must run. His face went blank with the foreknowledge, but his voice was as even as the chief's.

'The chief has spoken well,' he said. 'Only in one particular is he in error. I did not kill Running Fawn, nor did I speak with her after that first meeting in the sight of all. As for the knife, I had thrown it away. Someone who hates me must have found it.'

They listened, but as he had known, no one believed. Denial was to be expected. He would acquire stature in their eyes by an acknowledgment of guilt. But at least he'd show them that he was still a mountain man.

'I have nothing more to say. If *one* must die instead of many being slain in battle, I reckon it's better that way. I can't prove that I didn't kill her. Talk it over—and I'll be waiting and ready when the time comes.'

They heard him in silence. Moccasins stirred the dust uneasily, for it had been a long night and this was a bitter dawn. No need to tell a mountain man what this meant. An Indian was a funny creature. At times he could rise to a nobility that shamed a white man, and Big Eagle had exemplified forbearance and a desire for justice rather than vengeance.

But when that was said, an Indian was not a white man. Once they had their victim, they would exact a full measure of vengeance upon him, and the thought of how that would be done made the strongest stomachs turn queasy, and caused cold sweat to break on faces. It was an unseemly thing to give a white man up to torture.

Against that was the grim certainty that scores must die, many as horribly, if they refused to yield him up. And Irons had taken the need of decision from them by agreeing to go. He had proclaimed his innocence, but only a handful took that seriously.

There was the knife. Everyone had seen him take it away from the man called Clubfoot. And now it turned up, stuck in the girl's heart. Murder was hard to argue away.

To top it, there was the price of plews, the sell-out of every trapper, red or white. Big Eagle had made a mighty convincing argument on that point, as had the other chief before him. Winters and the long cold never stopped coming, and no man could brush aside the need for fur when the blizzards howled. Contrary talk was foolishness.

Bird song swelled, but ears were stoppered against it. Anyhow it seemed out of place. In this dawn, men were cold sober, but the hang-over was mean and sharp.

There had been dignity, and it must be matched. There was no unseemly haste. Men talked, and a few gathered about Irons, questioning, assuring him of their belief. And drifted away. He looked for Shawneen, wondering where he prowled. The sun burst across the Green, but nothing was changed.

Irons waited with a stoicism that matched the Indians', while the forms were observed and time ran out. He'd been captive to Indians before, up in the Milk River country. A broad land, the valley of the Milk. And the water was better than the hue indicated. He'd had rich trapping, that winter, but the Blackfeet had traded his plews to the Hudson's Bay.

Still, he'd never counted that as a loss, considering, for luck had been with him before that episode was played out. That was a background of experience to steady the nerves now. And they needed it. This time, he had no hope of luck.

A few people still slept here and there, strain and exhaustion and intoxication taking their toll. As the bird song died, silence reclaimed the big camp. Cooking fires were yet to be kindled, and no voices were raised as on ordinary mornings. Everything waited on him—and as the last muttered voices dwindled in the common silence, he walked a score of paces to where Big Eagle stood.

The chief, surrounded by fellow-dignitaries of the other tribes, was clothed in majesty. Still in silence, they closed around him and the procession moved off, across the Green. They stalked through the Indian camp, squaws and braves and children, old men and boys, surrounding, spreading out like the tail of a dragging kite.

Footsteps flailed the earth. A voice rose in argument; there was a sharp scuffle, and Shawneen burst through and up to Irons. His rage was like a spark in dry grass, communicating itself to the others.

'Yo're a crazy set!' he shouted. 'You think if he'd stuck that knife in her, he'd a been so big a fool as to leave it to be found?'

That was logic which the others had overlooked, or, if it had occurred to them, they had avoided mentioning it. But the time for logic was past. Interference only angered the Indians; Shawneen's insistence on going with Irons further enraged them. Irons, helpless to aid him, saw his friend dragged along.

'What'd you have to get in it for?' he demanded, and knew the answer before it was forthcoming.

'We been in a lot o' things together.'

Shawneen's voice was stubborn. 'This mule ain't leavin' you to go it alone.'

*   *   *

Rowena, opening her eyes, was conscious of a wrongness about the day. Sunshine upon the tent seemed mocking, the silence of the hour was alien, and the fear of the night was grown monstrous and smothering. She sat up, crying out to Lexie, yet keeping her voice hushed.

'What is it?' Lexie awoke disheveled, the same evidences of uneasy slumber in her reddened eyes. 'What's happened?'

'I don't know,' Rowena confessed. 'But oh, Lexie, I had a horrible dream!'

'Dreams are only dreams,' Lexie said reassuringly. 'Tell me what it was and then forget it.'

'It's too terrible even to talk about.' Rowena shuddered. 'Let's get outside and see what's happening. Somehow this silence frightens me, too.'

'It must be all right,' Lexie repeated. 'At least there's no fighting or any sort of disturbance.'

'There's nothing,' Rowena whispered, as they stepped outside. 'Look! Nothing is going on—no cooking fires, no trading. Men aren't even talking. It's as if—as if they were dead!'

'They're alive enough,' Lexie protested, but she knew what Rowena meant. And across the river, though the tepees stood as before, that portion of the camp seemed even more silent and deserted.

Rowena headed for the nearest group of trappers. On the previous day drinking had been the main occupation, but now, though a couple of jugs stood by a tree, no one seemed interested in them.

They were disinclined to talk, but gradually Rowena drew from them a recital of what had happened while she slept. They had been discussing an added piece of news, of a pattern with the rest, and as it had come last in sequence, she learned it first.

'Jim Hammond, dead in the tradin' tepee,' one growled. 'Two dead, for the matter o' that. Looks like that renegade Clubfoot snuck up an' used another knife on him! But Hammond was like a weasel—he looked sort o' slim an' puny, but he could outfight wildcats. Fooled that renegade, plenty.'

It was horrible news, difficult to assess or evaluate. But the other, when she drew it from reluctant lips, drove even that horror from her mind.

'Merciful heavens!' she gasped, and would have fallen had it not been for Lexie's ready arm. 'You mean they've taken him—to punish him?'

'Irons an' Shawneen, yeah. That ol' mule's stubborn as a jack—as a critter like him can be. Should a knowed better than to interfere after things had started. Went pushin' and scrappin' to get through the Injuns an' jine Irons. He made it—but o' course they took him along. He's sort o' a pardner in everything.'

It was Lexie's turn to go pale.

'And they'll treat him—they'll treat them both the same?'

'Reckon so, ma'am.' The trapper stirred uneasily. White women were the devil in Indian country. Trouble followed them like a wolf on the hunger trail. It was mighty apparent here, since their coming. He was disapproving. Still, they were a right pretty pair, and distressed, as was easy to tell.

'Shawneen always was a cantankerous old fool,' he added. 'And you'll have to give 'em credit, they did the right thing. Irons wouldn't listen when some of us tried to talk him out of it. 'Course, he had the right. Guilty or not, it's better for one or two to die than for dozens to be killed. It had to be them. But say what you like, them two ain't cowards.'

'Killed?' Rowena repeated. 'Will they—will they torture them?'

The trapper looked uncomfortable.

'It won't be purty,' he conceded. 'Injuns—well, they sort of figger they got a wrong to right, as you might put it.'

'But what will they do?' Rowena persisted. 'I must know.'

'Knowin' ain't going to easy him any, or you.'

'I—I dreamed they had him a captive.' Rowena spoke like a sleepwalker, reciting by rote. 'It was that which woke me ... They had him and they—they were burning him at the stake!'

The mountain man shuffled uncomfortably.

'If there was ary thing we could do, 'thout startin' a war, we'd shore do it,' he argued hoarsely. 'Leastwise, some of us would. But them ol' coons knew what they'd git when they went.'

'You mean they *will* burn them?'

'They sure as blazes won't do nothin' less,' a second man growled, made uneasy by this persistence. 'That's the Injun way.'

CHAPTER TWELVE

It would be a slow business, made to last out the day. Irons knew that as he stalked between his guards, Shawneen pressing close like a faithful dog. There was comfort and hurt alike in such faithfulness. Since Shawneen had insisted on going along, they would give him the same treatment. The torment would be both lessened and increased by his sharing.

Their foes recognized them as brave men and paid tribute to their voluntary acceptance by refraining from the usual harassment. But such preliminaries were a small thing compared with the big show in which they would be the principals. Shawneen's voice was tight with anger.

'Strikes me we're a pair o' fools. Know what I found out?'

'What?' Irons was past curiosity, but Shawneen was a true friend.

'Higginson's more for fox than skunk. He done a heap of palaverin' as he passed out the whiskey. Fixed it up with everybody yesterday that they was to sell to us. An' git their pay. He told them we'd never take the fur back to St. Louis—never even move it out of camp. When we *didn't* take out the plews, Higginson was to get 'em for extry trade—at *half* of what we paid!'

Irons' feet stuck as if in deep mud. An Indian bumped against him, but he paid no heed. He'd supposed himself drained of emotion, of anger and fear, ready to do what must be done. But wrath surged through him as he understood.

Let them buy, and bankrupt the Mountain in the process. Higginson had planned a trap from the start. For half of what they paid—only a quarter of the original price—he intended to have all the fur!

Since the trappers would profit by receiving

half as much again as they had been told they'd have to take, making the final price not too much below the original, there had been plenty, redskinned and white, to accept the proposition.

Having made the compact with Higginson accounted for so many standing aloof during these later developments. Fear and shame and greed had kept them silent. Having once sold him out, it was doubly hard to draw back. And his death would complete the deal, giving them the plews for the second trading.

'They've sort of overlooked Hammond,' he pointed out.

'That snake Higginson don't miss nothin',' Shawneen growled. 'Jim's dead, with a knife in him. Clubfoot got him in his tent. Jim managed to kill the renegade in turn—but I reckon it was planned.'

Irons didn't doubt it. Guile had been apparent from the moment of their arrival. Getting rid of Jim Hammond was the final link. He'd been sent by Pete Burley to assure the success of the Mountain and, if possible, to compass the ruin of Parks and Higginson. He was doing just the opposite—because Rowena had betrayed him to Higginson.

And what a man she'd picked! But he couldn't blame her too much; she had been deceived. Now she'd be in the power of that cold-blooded schemer. And the worst of it was that he could do nothing. It was too late to turn back now, to try to talk to the Indians. They had been given their hour, but the last sand had spilled through the glass.

Had Shawneen thought to go to the other mountain men with what he had learned ... But he'd been frantic to get to his friend when he learned what was happening. In any case, it would probably have been useless.

Death would come harder, now, a last triumph for Higginson. None of the whites would be permitted to come near them, nor they to return or communicate. They were two among hundreds, and blood fever was rising as the sun, on what would be a day of blistering heat.

Higginson remained discreetly in the background as night gave way to day, a day in which the shadowy processes which he had set afoot began to walk. Save for a word dropped here and there in carefully chosen ears, this was now out of his hands. He was well content to have it so.

If only he could forget Running Fawn, and the way she had sagged, a dead weight, in his arms!

The two Peters, Irons and Burley, had been formidable opponents, but this time he'd outmatched them, thanks to Parks and Rowena. And the renegade, Clubfoot, had dealt with Hammond, who, if left alive, would have been as formidable as a roused grizzly.

While the night still held, Higginson had lifted the flap of the trader's tent and peered in, to be sure there had been no slip.

Shock had gripped him for an instant as he saw how retribution had overtaken the man with the hobnailed boots. But when he had lowered the flap and stolen away, he was smiling. It was better that way. A cowardly tongue could be a menace.

The death of Hammond rounded out his plan. No longer would the Mountain cast its shadow across the fur lands. Once this was ended, it would be flattened to a molehill.

There could be but one possible source of trouble now—Rowena. She would be angry if she learned even half of the devious paths he had followed. But he would know how to deal with her, as he was dealing with Irons.

It would be a pleasure to show her his mastery. But for her blundering in, Running Fawn would still be alive. Hate was a sharp stab, like the thrust of a knife.

He turned, annoyed, as Yosemite pushed aside the flap and entered unannounced and uninvited. Today he seemed more wizened than usual, the melancholy deeper in his eyes.

'Well, I reckon yo're tickled!' he said, and his voice was mocking. 'You sure worked it clever. The Injuns have got 'em now!'

'Would you rather they'd have you?' Higginson demanded. 'They wanted somebody. Better him than us.'

Yosemite held his nose in an unmistakable gesture.

'I was in Digger country once,' he said. 'I'd been lost in the desert a spell, and was starvin' till my backbone was rubbin' a hole through my belly. They treated me good as they knew how—fed me on rats an' snakes. It was only that I was so starved that I could go that diet. But for choice I reckon they's some things to be said for the Diggers.'

'What the devil do you mean?' Higginson was repressed, a man driven by fear, hagridden with guilt. Yosemite's voice was a taunt.

'Yeah, better him than us,' he mocked. 'The Injuns think they're going to roast the devil out of the man who killed Running Fawn. Which is one time when the red devils ain't half as smart as they think. *And mebby some others ain't, either!*' He grinned, and his leer was horrible. 'All they could see was that knife stickin' in her back. Looks like they plumb missed the marks on her throat!'

'What the devil do you mean?' Higginson repeated, his voice a snarl. But emotion was too strong in the little man to be checked. He was like a high diver in mid-air, sensing danger, but unable to turn back.

'She was long dead before the knife was stuck in her,' he said, and naked hate looked out of his eyes. 'Her paw would like to know why she was killed—and to get his fingers

164

twisted in the hair o' the man who did it!'

Twin rages motivated him. He had hankered for Running Fawn in his own tepee. Since her death he had bided his time, as a spider waits. Once death had claimed its prey, it could not be undone. Though hate roughened his voice, greed slurred his tones.

'I know when she was back in your tepee,' he added slyly. 'Likewise how you pushed her under the robes. You calc'late keepin' that between us is worth more to you than it would be to Big Eagle?'

It was not easy for Higginson to feel self-righteous, but in the presence of so contemptible a creature, he almost achieved it. Though coveting the girl, knowing what had happened to her, Yosemite had held himself in check, planning blackmail. He conceived this to be the moment, since a yell would fetch others on the run. He counted on that, a bravo in the daylight.

Fools never learned. That was why they were fools. Higginson had discovered how swift the stroke of a knife could be, how easily a dagger-pointed blade drove into flesh. Such knowledge could be useful, and he had provided himself with a knife similar in pattern to the red-handled one.

Yosemite sensed danger and tried to turn, too late. His staring eyes bulged and his mouth popped open, but there was no time even for the scream to rise in his throat before the thrust struck deep. He toppled sideways, away from the stroke, and a gush of red spilled after the withdrawn blade.

Higginson's glance darted nervously. The actual killing had been easy, but it was day again, and for a second time he had a body to dispose of.

But experience was a good teacher. The buffalo robes made a good cover, and no one who came would be the wiser. Even Yosemite had come into the tepee and stood to palaver the day before while the heavy skins concealed their secret.

Cleansing the knife, Higginson stepped out into the sunshine. The bad part had been remembering, thinking of Running Fawn. He'd be long in getting over her. Aside from that, it was as an old mountain man had told him: The first killing came hard, and made your stomach squeamish. But it soon got to be a habit.

★   ★   ★

Confirmation concerning Irons was on every face. It was unnecessary to ask anyone else, though Rowena questioned several. One thing she learned which was a step removed from hopelessness; the Indians would not hurry with despatching their victims. They would savor the show, prolonging it and life to the last possible moment.

'And a man can die mighty slow, even by fire,' one trapper grunted, his face blank with stirred memory. 'I know. I've seen 'em.'

Her determination that something must be done grew stronger as the obstacles increased. None of these men, even those who counted Irons as a friend, would do more than shake their heads. Most of them figured it as out of the question, taken from their hands. Irons had given himself up voluntarily, and that argued guilt, despite his denial. 'Course, it was right unpleasant to think about, but—

There was one man who might be able to do something. It was natural that she should turn to him, since she had journeyed so far to join him. Already, for his sake, she had sacrificed much. But because of that, he could not refuse what she asked.

Higginson was likely enough in his tepee. Leastwise, no one had seen him for a spell.

'Talk to them, Lexie!' Rowena appealed frantically. 'There must be *someone* among them who will at least try to do something. I'll find Paul.'

She fled across the campground, dodging between tepees, skirting trees and brush, giving no thought to what would have checked her even a day earlier, the impropriety of seeking Higginson out in his own tepee. Breathless, she cried his name and, when there was no response, snatched aside the flap. There was a faint stirring, as though he might be just awakening.

Or perhaps he was rousing from the stupor of drink of the night before. But he should be sober now.

She peered about uncertainly in the half-light. The tepee was empty. But the sound came again. Rowena called, hearing the quaver in her voice.

A groan was her answer. She looked about, bewildered, then, with sudden understanding, jerked up the corner of the heavy buffalo robes. They had been well-tanned, worked soft and pliable by the patient toil of squaws. But the coarse black hair was long and heavy, the weight of a single robe burdensome.

She started back, almost dropping the robe again, then steadied. Her fear for Paul vanished in a measure of relief at discovering a stranger. But this other man was hurt. Throwing the covers entirely back, she dropped to her knees, touching his side, and her fingers came away sticky with blood. For all that, his eyes were open, bright with some emotion that transcended pain.

'What—who did this?' she gasped. Seeing the nature of the wound, it was easy to tell how he had been struck down.

'Him—Hig.' Yosemite's voice was a croak, so that she had to bend close. 'He was—scared that I'd tell on him. Which I would.'

168

'What do you mean?' Rowena held her voice steady.

'Running Fawn was with him when you reached camp,' Yosemite explained, and a fixed and terrible resolution fought to hold back dissolution until he had finished. 'She was Hig's squaw. He made her—play that trick on Irons. When she wouldn't give him up—he killed her. Stuck that knife—into her. She—was in the way. Then—because I knew—he knifed me—'

He could manage no more, but there was no need. As he sank back, Rowena came slowly to her feet. Mechanically she pulled back the robes, covering him again. Then, blinded as if by the glare, she moved out into the sunshine.

CHAPTER THIRTEEN

On this side of the Green men gathered in little groups, impelled to companionship, but they did not talk. It was a soberness worse than hang-over. Across the river the tepees pointed crooked fingers at an empty sky, flaps moving emptily in a whisper of breeze. All who had thronged the encampment had gone into the woods, mingling without distinction as to tribe, beginning the business of the day.

A scream lifted hysterically in Rowena's

169

throat, but she choked it down, knuckles pressed hard against her mouth. There was still time—there had to be. Now she had a weapon in her hands, but she must use it skillfully. He who trapped the fox dared not bungle like one who set only a snare for rabbits.

It was a hot day, with the threat of worse to come. For the first time, Rowena saw many things clearly, and was sickened by the narrowness of her own escape from a man who would so use a fellow creature to further his own ends.

The guilt was Higginson's, and his alone. But the responsibility for what had happened was equally upon her own head, because of the secret which she had betrayed to him.

Because of what she had done, Irons was going to his death. She saw clearly now. Irons was making this sacrifice to insure against a savage outbreak which would mean widespread slaughter. He was doing it because he loved her!

Greater love hath no man, than to lay down his life. But what of the love of a woman for her man? On that point she had refused to think, drawing back at the misconception of duty. But her heart had known all along. Irons was her man, and she loved him.

There was no one to turn to—no one except Higginson. She had two weapons, and one or both must be made to serve her need, no matter what the cost. Off in the distance she saw him, and drawing up her skirts, she broke into a run.

Higginson saw her coming, and waited. The reaction of dealing with Yosemite had passed, and he had control of himself. This meeting with Rowena might be unpleasant, for he could guess her purpose. But let her ask. It might be turned to his own ends.

As she ran, Rowena strove to order her thoughts, to plan. It wouldn't do to let Higginson know that she understood the depths of his evil—at least not yet. Yosemite had made that mistake and found, too late, that he no longer dealt with an ordinary man. The Indians had a name for such a creature, an explanation. They believed that sometimes the spirit of a wolf entered into the body of a man—*a windigo*—

That notion seemed like fancy or fantasy, except for being so horribly accurate. But whatever it was, she must deal with him. Rowena reined tightly against bucking emotions, but at least there was no need to conceal her agitation.

'Paul!' she exclaimed. 'What is this I hear—about Mr. Irons? What are they going to do?'

Higginson did not pretend ignorance.

'I'm sorry this has happened, my dear,' he said carefully. 'Doubly so on your account. It's true that the Indians have him. It's too bad, in a way. But look at it sensibly, Rowena. They caught him red-handed, so he's only getting what he deserves.'

'But there must be some mistake.' Rowena strove to keep revulsion from her voice. 'I understand that he gave himself up, voluntarily, to protect the rest of us.'

Higginson's laugh was like the bark of a wolf.

'Voluntarily? I tell you they had him dead to rights, and he knew it. He must have thought he could get away with anything—that a squaw didn't count. Perhaps he might have done so, ordinarily. But after coming here with the news of a price cut and enraging everyone, it was just too much.'

'But it wasn't he who gave out that news,' she reminded him.

Higginson shrugged. 'What does it matter? He brought the news, the orders, and he had to accept the responsibility when they put it up to him. Rightly or wrongly, they blame him. Piled on top of this other—'

Rowena ignored the mockery. She saw that he would argue interminably, hedging in the situation with a forest of words. She cut through desperately.

'None of that matters now. What does count is that he is one of us—a white man. This must be stopped.'

'I know what you mean. We all feel the same way. But what can we do? These are mountain men here—and they are as hardy a race as the world has known. We might aptly compare them with the Vikings, or the Pilgrims, or perhaps the men who settled Ohio and Kentucky. These trappers walk the same rough trails. And don't forget, they hate Indians. That is schooled in them, as the main issue of survival. You have only to look to see how this gripes them. But they realize that it's justice; also that nothing can be done.'

'*You* can do something,' Rowena said, and played her first card. '*You* are not an ignorant mountaineer, Paul, but a leader. Do it for me, Paul. Save him.'

The simplicity of her plea made it devastating. Higginson managed a crooked, little-boy smile.

'You put me on a pedestal, Rowena,' he said, sighing. 'I wish I were half the man you think me. You'd have me upon a mountain before I've ever climbed it.'

'Will you?' she persisted.

He shook his head. 'I can't. Believe me, I'd do anything for you, my dear. But when it came to the showdown, Irons was right. He knew they'd demand a sacrifice. I suppose there was a bit of nobility in him, at the last. Even a squaw man has his moments.'

Fury tore away her control.

'You beast!' Her voice shrilled. 'You are the squaw man! Running Fawn was your woman, and everyone knows it. Then you turned upon her and killed her, because I had come and she was in your way! After that, you murdered Yosemite to shut him up! I found him dying, in your tepee, and he told me! Now, will you murder *me?* Try—and I'll scream the truth for everyone to hear! What do you think they'll do to you then?'

Higginson's face blotched. His eyes darted to the mountain men, lounging in small groups, their faces heavy with restraint. They were near enough to hear a shout, or to see if he struck at her. His effort at control made a rattle in his throat.

'I don't know what you mean,' he protested. 'There's been an awful mistake somewhere, Rowena. But of course you're overwrought. I know what a shock this has been to you, so I don't blame you. But surely you don't believe the things you've been saying?'

There could be no turning back. Her answer was devastatingly simple.

'I've seen a rattlesnake in coil. If one talked for a thousand years, I couldn't be convinced that it was anything other than the horror it is.'

'Then, why don't you tell what you think? Why don't you throw me to the wolves, if that's the way you feel? You can gloat while they roast *me* at the stake! If that's the measure of your love and devotion, go ahead!'

The flicker of fear in his eyes belied the words. Rowena saw it, and her own were implacable. This was her last weapon.

'I will, if I have to. But I'll give you one chance. You've contrived this whole affair, and you can undo it. Save Irons, and you save yourself.'

Higginson had control of himself again. The leader of a wolf pack must be crafty. Courage coupled with experience might bring one to the pinnacle, but it took more than those to hold it.

'You're wrong, Rowena,' he protested. 'Wrong all the way. But this is no time to try to explain. It's an awful gamble that you're asking me to take, and I'll do my best, for your sake. But I've got to have something in return—as a guarantee of your good faith. Besides, it's the only chance I can see that might possibly work.'

'What do you mean?'

'I mean that the Indians are mad. They've got a victim and they're thirsting for his blood. Along with the rest, they want a show. It will take something out of the ordinary to break in on them now, to get and hold their attention. But if we give them another show—a big enough one—we may manage that far. And as a climax to it, I may be able to talk them out of killing Irons. I'll tell them that it was a mistake—that it was Yosemite who killed Running Fawn. The old chief knows that he wanted her, so that will seem reasonable.'

They would have to have a victim, of course, and Yosemite was dead. Nothing could hurt him now.

'Wouldn't it be more convincing if you went to them and told them that you'd found Yosemite was guilty, and had killed him?'

Higginson shook his head. 'It wouldn't work. They want a show. If we give them the right kind, and then I tell them—and ask a boon for you as my bride—maybe they'll let Irons go. It's the only chance I can think of.'

Rowena felt cold. 'What do you mean?' she managed.

'I'll get the friar to marry us, with the Indians watching. It will be an impressive ceremony—the sort of show they like. That way, maybe they won't feel too cheated. It's the only chance I can see.'

He'd warned her that he must have a guarantee of her good faith. Becoming his wife would be that guarantee. But Irons' life was at stake, through her own bungling.

'I'll do anything,' she agreed, 'so that you save him. But if you don't, I'll make sure that you suffer the same fate.'

'I'll do my best,' Higginson repeated. 'Don't let me down; we'll all be in his shoes if we start this thing and don't carry it through. Now wait at your tent. I'll hurry things as fast as I can. The red devils won't be far along, yet. They make an elaborate business of it. But I'll rush.'

There was a haze in the sky, but despite it, the heat of the day was becoming oppressive. Even so, Rowena was increasingly cold as she returned to her tent. Perhaps something as highly dramatic as Higginson had proposed was the only chance, with the situation so far advanced. Higginson had not said so, but he would do nothing unless assured that her silence was purchased, that he would be rewarded.

But she had the nagging fear that she had done the wrong thing. She should have cried out to the trappers, explaining everything, trusting to them. Now, warned and desperate, Higginson was doubly wary. Despite her threat of exposure, she mistrusted him exactly as she had said.

As a last resort, she could still denounce him. The trouble was, that might not save Irons. Many of the trappers were no friends of his. Some of them were craven in the shadow of the stake. Others worshipped the same god as Higginson—money. It was to their advantage to get Irons out of the way, for only then would half of their trade loss be returned.

The tent was empty. She had hoped for Lexie. Never had she felt so alone.

She was not kept waiting long. On that part of his promise, at least, Higginson made

177

good. Despite the hampering robes, Don Diego came almost at a run.

'Higginson sent me to bring you,' he explained. 'He's arranging for the Indians to take time off to witness the ceremony. We'd better hurry.'

'Very well.' She sought to match his long stride, reflecting that never before had she seen him other than modishly indolent. 'But this—this is a mockery!'

'Do you think I'd take part in it otherwise? I once cherished the hope, Rowena, of wedding you myself—but never to another man!'

In the stress of other emotions she had temporarily forgotten that part. Don Diego was no priest. But once the words were mumbled over them, she would be in Higginson's power . . .

'I'm not doing it for any love of Higginson!' she said.

Don Diego slowed his pace. His look was long and searching, tinged with pity.

'My poor child!' he murmured. 'Your eyes are open at last, aren't they?'

She was too distraught for subterfuge, too breathless to do more than nod.

'So it's Irons!' he added. 'I guessed as much. I think you've chosen well. I loved you, Rowena—but you saw me for what I was. I don't understand how, with such insight, you were fooled by Higginson. Ah, well. Now, you're willing to sacrifice yourself to save Irons.'

'Could I do any less—after betraying him?'

'Perhaps not. It's curious, Rowena, but I begin to understand. As I believe I told you once, it must be these robes. They were worn by a good man, and they represent an ideal. And following that vein of thought, it's true that most of the Indians, if they don't believe in the Black Robes, at least respect them. Some of them feel a superstitious awe. I really believe that Higginson has a clever idea. This sort of thing will catch and turn their attention when nothing else would be likely to.'

She made no reply, and he went on earnestly:

'We will strive to make it succeed! But remember that as a ceremony it has no meaning. Whether he knows it or not, you and I do. I'm no more a priest of the church than you are one of their sisterhood. Whatever I do will have no legal sanction from the state, no spiritual blessing from the church. It will be only a bit of mummery —but play your part! There was a time when I fancied myself as an actor. Today we shall see.'

She did not fully understand, and it was strange but there was comfort in the words of this man whom she had feared and hated. She looked at him curiously, and her glance surprised something in his eyes before he turned them quickly away. Twice he'd mocked that something of the sanctity which was supposed to attach to the robes he wore might have rubbed off on him. She had scoffed at such a notion, but now she wondered. Certainly he played a new role in more ways than one.

There was time for no more talk. They were beyond the deserted Indian camp, abruptly in the green of trees. Not far ahead was an opening, a large natural meadow. Rowena remembered it from two days before—was it only that long since they had arrived at the rendezvous? It seemed like half a span of life. Their trail had skirted the clearing. Sounds told that the Indians were there.

Higginson joined them. His glance swept Rowena's face and seemed satisfied.

They reached a smaller adjacent meadow. Only a thin fringe of brush and trees separated it from the larger, and through them she glimpsed a huge stake, set deep. Standing with his back to it, contemptuously erect, was Irons. She could see no more, as other brush intervened.

Higginson's prestige with the Indians was at a new high. He had not been popular in the past, being too shrewd a tradesman. But since the coming of Irons they considered him to be on their side. He had been generous with whiskey, for which he received no barter, and with promises to get them extra money for their plews.

So he had gained their ear without too much trouble. And in what was about to transpire the robe of the friar was potent medicine. Higginson had explained to the chiefs, and his wish prevailed. A hush settled over the meadow, and the braves and squaws, the children and the old men, all trooped to this smaller space and waited expectantly.

The reaching pines were like the nave of a great church, faintly dappled with sunlight falling through. That part reminded Rowena of Notre Dame in Paris, but there the similarity ended. This was like a walking nightmare, and the tense savages were proof that they were deep within a wilderness. Beyond, just out of sight and hearing, Peter Irons was shackled to the post which was intended to be his pyre.

Her only chance now was to trust Don Diego. Higginson had fooled her twice. But somehow, trusting this man who wore the black robe was no longer so ridiculous.

A member for life of his church, even if rarely a devout son, Don Diego had ever an eye for detail and a retentive memory. There were variations, but he made an impressive ritual of the ceremony which at least satisfied and impressed the audience to which they played. It was at the culmination, as he raised his hands as if for the blessing, that he stepped out in his own right upon this macabre stage.

A man fluent of tongue, speaking at least four languages, in this moment Don Diego had no knowledge of any tribal dialect. But many of the Indians knew some English, and in that he was as apt as in his native Castilian.

'Hear me,' he intoned. 'I of the Black Robe speak to you, to all. I speak the truth. Listen, Big Eagle, Chief of the Pawnees, father of Running Fawn. You have been fooled by one who uses you for his own evil purposes. Running Fawn was killed, but whose squaw was she? You know, Big Eagle. You had given her to Higginson, who wished to cast her aside for this white woman, whom now he tries also to force to his will. Running Fawn was Higginson's squaw, but she was a woman of high spirit. When she refused to be cast away, he killed her. Many of you know Irons from the past, and you know him for a man who speaks straight, who has no squaw in any camp.

'I tell you this: Irons is your friend. The man who killed Running Fawn stands here. Seize him, and I will prove it.'

Surprise momentarily held everyone spellbound, including Higginson. He had bowed his head in mock humility for the blessing, but he jerked it up incredulously. It took a moment longer for the Indians to understand, but there could be no question of their reaction. He had planned an elaborate mummery to impress them and to put Rowena completely in his power, so that she could not denounce him.

But Don Diego had become suddenly the main actor, carrying this beyond any plan of Higginson's. He was the Black Robe, and he had built to a climax. They would heed his words.

Higginson was a wolf cornered but not yet trapped. He turned, jerking at his pistol, his face livid.

Big Eagle saw Higginson's intent and leaped at him. The pistol flamed, and the Pawnee wavered like a tree shaken in the wind. His outreaching hands closed on emptiness, then Higginson darted back among the trees.

Don Diego's hands had been raised in the gesture of benediction. Now they dropped, and in a quick gesture he swept aside the robes, to snatch at a fancy dueling pistol, silver-mounted but no less deadly. Somehow there was nothing incongruous in the change of role.

But he was too late. Higginson was out of sight, while the chief writhed on the ground, and a rumble of anger stirred the throng as they understood. Still clutching the gun, Don Diego reached with his other hand and caught Rowena's wrist.

'Come!' he commanded, and headed at a trot back for camp. 'Irons will be all right,' he added, 'But we'll be better off on the other side of the Green until the excitement subsides. And I need to explain to the trappers before there's a misunderstanding.'

The situation had been explosive the night before, until it had taken an unexpected turn with the discovery of Running Fawn's body. It was equally dangerous now. The Indians were not angry with the mountain men, but they were sure enough mad. A few vented feelings in the gobble of a war whoop. Mountain men, hearing, and equally tense and frustrated, might not understand.

'Don Diego,' Rowena gasped, 'you were right. I mean about the robe.'

His thin face softened.

'Thank you, my dear,' he said. 'It is an amazing garment, this. But there is much of the devil in me still. Which is perhaps a good thing. As soon as we set the trappers straight, I shall lay aside the robe. It would be hampering when I am in a hurry, besides being unfitting for the task ahead.' He glanced at the pistol, still clutched so tightly that his knuckles showed white, and Rowena had no trouble in understanding. Unless the Indians were ahead of him, he intended to settle with Higginson.

There was a slight noise, so muffled by the excitement behind as to pass unnoticed. It was the twang of a bowstring released. The pistol plowed a furrow among dead leaves as Don Diego fell headlong, his arms outstretched. His fingers loosened upon her wrist, but not before he had almost jerked Rowena off her feet.

Higginson darted from a clump of brush, and Rowena turned belatedly to run.

In one hand, Higginson clutched a bow, a fancy weapon upon which some warrior had expended a lot of care. Well-seasoned, the wood had been stained, then wound at both ends and the middle with sinews of varied hues. In its own way, both for deadliness and show, it matched the pistol in the dirt.

With a jerk Higginson pulled her about and was running, leading the way deeper among the trees.

'If you try to yell, you'll wish you hadn't,' he warned. 'You're useful to me alive, but if you get in the way, you'll get the same treatment.'

The clamor behind them rose, then subsided as they made their way unmolested.

'That fool of a friar should have known better than to try and double-cross me!' Higginson muttered. 'But he'll serve a purpose. The trappers will see that arrow. Let the Indians try and explain it. They'll never be given a chance. And the more both bunches fight among themselves, the better for me!'

CHAPTER FOURTEEN

The first hour of captivity had not been too bad. Shawneen and Irons had known what to expect. Insults and small annoyances were inevitable. But their captors, thinking of a hot-spirited woman whose feet would never run again with the lightness of a fawn, would make sure that no great harm came to them until the day grew old.

Following the planting of the stakes, squaws and children had enlivened the time by gathering brush, well dried, scouring the surrounding woods. Mixed with it was wood not so seasoned, which would burn slowly. It was stacked in two piles, ready to put to use when the word was given. Watching these preparations for their own warming was calculated to flesh a man's nerves as flint scraped a pelt.

Respite was unexpected. Something drew the crowd, pulling them strongly. It would require an event out of the ordinary to get them away, while excitement was like fever in the blood. They exchanged glances, Shawneen shifting position as much as the rawhide which cut into his wrists permitted.

'Kinda funny, them leavin' us a-tall,' Shawneen observed. ''Twon't last though. One side o' me says I could stand a long spell o' delay. 'Tother's like a beaver, knowin' it's caught and going to be knocked in the head. Easier to get it over with.' He spat meditatively. 'Cur'us. Never did think much about them critters before. Now I got kind of a feller feelin' for the pore little devils. Mebby it's a good thing this is final. It could sort of rooin a man for his job.'

'So could this,' Irons retorted. Many things were in his mind, but it was not a time for words. He twisted, trying to see, as commotion broke out among the spectators. Whatever the new show was about, it had taken an unlooked-for turn. The sound of fury had run in his ears too many times to be misunderstood.

'They're squallin' worse'n a pack o' wildcats,' Shawneen sighed. 'Makes me itchy.'

The sudden excitement was abating, as quickly as it had begun. A chief's voice gave stern orders. That any good could come of this, Irons doubted, fearful of admitting even faint hope, yet conscious of its strong leap in his blood. He had taken this step deliberately, knowing what it meant. Had anyone called it courageous, he would have contradicted the assumption. It was something which must be.

A dozen warriors came back into sight. They carried an injured man, and when they reached the stakes they held him upright. It was Big Eagle, and the name was fitting.

Blood made a spreading stain above his heart, dripping and soaking the finery of holiday regalia. The others assisted him to stand, but will power alone kept his head erect and his voice steady as he addressed Irons.

'We have made a mistake,' he said, using his own tongue. 'The trader brought the white woman, to take her for his squaw. The Black Robe spoke words above them. But the Black Robe had courage. He told me, when all were assembled to hear, that it was the trader, not you, who killed Running Fawn. Whereat the trader shot me and escaped. Then he killed the Black Robe and fled, taking the white woman with him.'

Big Eagle rested a moment, gathering strength, while Irons listened in surprise. Then he went on:

'I have restrained the anger of the warriors. But while the trader remains at large he can cause much mischief. I dare not set our braves after him now. Later, when the men of your blood understand, then all may join in the hunt.' He looked at Shawneen. 'He can go to them and explain. But you will want to go after the trader, who has your woman.'

His reasoning was sound. The warriors were in a state of frenzy, and plenty of the mountain men would be in the same dangerous mood. If the Indians were turned loose now to spread wide in a hunt for Higginson, their purpose would be misunderstood, and a clash would be certain.

That, as the chief had sensed, was what Higginson was counting on. In such confusion, his own chances for escape would be improved. But until the matter was set straight in everyone's mind, the lull would also work for Higginson. If he was to be stopped, it was up to Irons.

A warrior cut him loose, and another handed him a rifle. Big Eagle, his duty done, sank wearily to the ground.

'Git him!' Shawneen encouraged, as they freed him. 'But watch yore step! He's the kind that don't rattle! I won't waste time settin' them other hosses straight,' he added.

A runner came, panting, as much from frustration as haste.

'Trader take canoe, go downriver,' he said. 'Girl with him, tied.'

That Higginson would steal a canoe was a measure of his desperation. He would know by now that somewhere his plan had miscarried, that there was at least a delay in the clash he'd hoped to engender between white men and red. But he could hardly guess that Big Eagle would have either the strength or the foresight to hold back his own warriors as he had done.

If Higginson had known, with the leeway it afforded, he would almost surely have taken horses. The Green, downstream from the rendezvous, was no highway to freedom. But with the odds precariously balanced, it might be a way to escape.

Irons reached the river, plunging through the deserted Indian encampment, his goal one of the remaining canoes.

A canoe was still drawn up on the bank, but its bottom had been kicked in. The log which spanned the gorge had been picked up and dropped, so there was no longer a bridge. There was a single remaining canoe, but it was on the opposite shore.

There was no mountain man handy to fetch it across to him. Apparently they had drawn back, watchful and suspicious, but in a mood to steer clear of trouble.

The banks pushed together, crowding the river, and the current changed from placidity to turbulence. But it was no great feat to swim across. Irons launched the canoe, dipping the paddle like a frightened beaver.

The first gorge, which ran through part of the camp, was short and easy. Below it the Green again widened, with willows dipping their branches in a pool. But this was only a breather. Almost at once the current quickened, sending the canoe leaping like a scared pony. The river made a long U and straightened again, and at the far end of the opening Irons sighted a craft, bobbing wildly amid white water.

It swept around another bend and out of sight, but it was likely that Higginson had seen him coming. Warned, he'd be twice as dangerous. Irons' paddle bent in his hands.

This was water to try the skill and courage of any boatman. The glassily smooth surface was deceptive. The current was driving the boat at a terrific speed, hurling it suddenly among frothing rapids, where boulders reared angrily, fighting an endless battle with the water. They tore it to shreds, making it boil with fury. In this mood of eternal combat, river and stones alike were always ready to turn on any interloper that dared come between.

Even this was not the worst. Around the next bend, at the foot of another long sweep, was the waterfall. Irons had explored this section and knew what it was like. Just short of the fall, rocky cliffs hemmed the river on both sides, forcing it to the plunge. No boat could go over and fail to splinter.

A good canoeman could beach his craft short of the falls, just where the cliffs began. At that point Higginson would have to take to the shore.

Given a bit more time, he must have planned to land and portage to the calmer waters below the falls, then continue his flight. If he had gotten that far, it would be difficult to overtake or stop him. With Rowena for a hostage, he was making a calculated gamble.

Irons was scarcely aware of the boulders

flashing past, of his own instinctive actions to avoid them. The canoe shaved destruction not merely by a razor's edge; it was an edge honed to split a hair. Objects on shore blurred with speed and the wash of spray. He rounded a bend, and the teeth of the cliff showed bared and snarling, a quarter of a mile below.

He'd tried to foresee what Higginson might do and plan against it. His expectation was that Higginson would have landed and be waiting to bushwhack him. For that reason it would be necessary to turn inshore at once, long before the best part of an unfriendly bank could be reached.

Farther down, the river was clear of the froth and the granite upthrusts. But here he must weave and twist between the boulders, a task calling as much for luck as skill. The intangibles, the hazards both visible and hidden, were too many to be judged and acted upon in the time allotted.

The high-flung mist, which had been blinding farther upstream, was gone. He could see clearly, and terror palsied his hands as he understood. Sanderson Parks had chosen a clever partner, a man as ruthless as he was adroit. Higginson had done the unexpected, and like a card player with access to a stacked deck, he seemed now to hold all the trumps in his hands.

Higginson's plan was simple. Having run

the white water safely, he had made his landing, close above the granite jaws of the river. On the shore, conveniently at hand, a finger of stone thrust up nearly as high as a man, weathered smooth and round.

With a rope, Higginson had taken a turn about the stone. The hemp was fastened to the end of the canoe, holding it a few feet out from shore. The frustrated current tugged relentlessly, and if the rope loosened, the canoe would leap like a frightened colt. Down below, the roar of the waterfall was a thunderous, unending throb.

Rowena lay in the bottom of the canoe, tied hand and foot.

Higginson stood in full view on the shore, rifle in one hand, rope's end in the other. This was surer than aiming a bushwhack bullet at Irons. If the mountain man came too close, he had only to let go of the rope. Should Irons try to shoot, he might score—but the bullet must kill Rowena as surely as it hit Higginson. If injured or killed, he would automatically let go of the life line.

Irons understood as well as if Higginson had told him in detail. He was to stand back and allow Higginson to pull the canoe in, then to make the portage around the falls and launch it again, without molestation. Rowena would be taken along.

Part of the price would be to smash his own canoe, so that he could not follow.

Running Fawn had died at Higginson's hands, yet Irons suspected that the man had loved her. That proof of ruthlessness became now his strongest trump. There would be no haggling, no compromise.

Whether a remnant of liking for Rowena remained, or whether all emotion had turned to hate in him, made scant difference. Life had become cheap in his eyes—all except his own. Now he had left no alternative.

So he figured, and so it seemed. Whether Rowena would prefer a quick and final end to going on in the power of this man was beside the point. That was not for Irons to judge. If it came to a showdown, he couldn't risk her life, and on that Higginson was making his gamble.

The element of surprise was grim, and as Higginson had hoped, it played into his hands. Irons' attention was riveted on the canoe and its helpless passenger. His arms were momentarily suspended, and in that instant his craft nudged a jagged edge of stone and buoyancy was sliced out of it. Irons spilled into the water.

His gun was gone with the boat. But in that moment when Higginson must feel assured that the victory was his, Irons felt no panic of the river, no frantic desire to scramble for the shore. He'd been given a new chance—a long one, with no lessening of hazard. But it was a chance.

Unhampered by the rifle, he could swim easily. Not much effort was required, for the current would carry him, and the boulder field was now behind and upstream. The trick would be to drift with the current, to keep submerged so that the lynx-eyed man behind the finger of stone would not spot him as he came. If he could reach the canoe—

Irons had no plan beyond that point, save the weapon which Higginson had used against him—surprise. He'd be hampered in holding the canoe from starting its final plunge, tugging it to shore in the face of a man with a gun. But let him get his hands on it, and try and stop him!

Back in St. Louis it would be full summer, and dogs would loll in the shade with panting tongues. Even the wide Missouri, slumberous and languid after its spring turbulence, would be taking on the feel of the sun. But here beyond the mountains, summer was still more a word than a reality. The snowbanks of the Rockies still fed the Green, and its waters were only hours removed from ice. It was fine water for beavers, making for prime plews over a long season. For a man it was harsh and bitter, and the sodden weight of his clothes made it worse.

Irons dared not kick or splash. The current was like a race horse now, settled to the stretch. Brush and trees and rearing stones along the shore had become live things, fleeing upstream, while the craggy jaws of the canyon opened wider at his approach.

With half the distance gone, Irons had a glimpse of Higginson, still clutching the rope end and the rifle, watchfully suspicious. A man in Indian country soon came to distrust the evidence of his eyes. He watched and waited and made doubly sure, or else he failed to live long enough to learn that lesson.

Higginson was unsure, but his eyes were on the river, and the rifle held ready. Either he'd seen something, or he was naturally wary.

Now a stretch of glassy water, the length which a stone might be flung, lay between. It was no great distance, measured in speed and time. Irons could make it almost in seconds, with the shoving current to aid. But it was a long way, with death waiting to pounce. The rifle spat like a hissing cat, and the bullet made a savage *chuk* in the waters, close beside his head. It was so near that Irons heard it before the noise of the gun reached him and his eyes saw the boil.

That took him by surprise. It was close—and very good shooting, under the circumstances. He raised his head quickly, knowing that Higginson would be handicapped with gun and rope together, that it took time to reload. This might be the moment. On the other hand, the hoped-for surprise was lost, and he faced a killer who'd drop the rope in an instant.

Higginson had let go the useless rifle. But now he fisted a pistol.

The current was relentless. From upstream, Irons had judged that the canoe swung close enough to the shore that he could make the bank with it. He could still do so, given the chance, though with scant leeway. But he could not halt his own progress or even do much to slow his speed. He had a choice of plunging shoreward, or going ahead. Either way, Higginson had only to bide his time, to shoot again when Irons presented a good target.

But he was thinking stupidly. Only an hour before, he'd been tied to a stake, amid a throng yelping for his blood. No gambler worth the name would have given odds on his chances, yet that crisis was one with all the past. He'd been in plenty of perilous situations, and lived to reach this one.

Now, it looked as if Higginson had won. That was good, because he'd be thinking the same, grown cocky by the times he'd skirted death and turned it to his own ends. And *he had only one shot in his pistol!*

Irons raised out of water in a quick, desperate plunge for the shore. He turned in the middle of the stroke and dived again, and the snarl of the gun sounded as he went under. Higginson had taken his bait, and missed.

Now Higginson would drop the rope.

Knowing the man, Irons had no doubts. But he would reach the canoe and snatch it back to safety. And if he had to fight, man to man, hampered as he'd be, still he'd win. Now the odds were his, and his blood, chill as the water a moment before, was singing.

He surfaced like a beaver, seeing the canoe start its leap, the rope trailing behind. Irons snatched and had it, close to the end. Jerk was strong, but he clung, plunging shoreward. He reached the bank and came out, braced for attack—and stared unbelieving.

Then, feeling the angry tug of the bobbing canoe, he pulled it in, hand over hand, drawing it up on the sand. He lifted Rowena, and seeing the look in her eyes, forgot all else. Her lips met his, responsive, but salty with tears.

Higginson had tied her tightly at wrists and ankles. The flung spray of the journey had wet the ropes, tightening them until the bonds were galling, the knots all but impossible. Irons lowered her on to the sand and turned. Higginson should have a knife.

A second time he looked at the man, sprawled with his face in the edge of the water. A steady ooze of red poured from his temple, making a faint stain in the current. Looking around, Irons saw the Indian.

Tall Man came toward him, one hand holding his rifle, the other uplifted in greeting, his boyish face stern but proud. Indians had a knack of choosing appropriate names. Big Eagle. Running Fawn. Tall Man. He was tall as he came.

That explained what had happened to Higginson. Irons lifted a hand in grave salutation, found the knife in a pocket, and cut Rowena loose. She stood up as the boy reached them, one hand on Irons' arm to steady herself. The other she reached toward the Comanche.

'That was well done, Tall Man,' she said. 'My thanks to you.'

'Tall Man happy,' the boy returned gravely. He accepted her hand, held it a moment. Then he looked at Irons, and admiration kindled a fire in his eyes. 'You not need help, at that,' he said.

'It was mighty welcome, and I did need it,' Irons assured him. 'But how did you manage? I didn't know you had reached the rendezvous, and I thought the chiefs were keeping all their warriors in check.'

Tall Man shrugged. 'Others, yes,' he agreed. 'Tall Man just arrive. Find what happen. Comanche not like others. Not bound by them.'

He'd raced downriver on horseback, and his arrival had been timely. Now he brought his horse.

'You ride,' he invited Rowena. 'We walk.'

Rowena hesitated as Irons turned to lift

her. 'I had to make you hate me,' she murmured. 'Or so I believed. I was so dreadfully wrong.'

'You could never make me hate you,' Irons said gently, and had recourse to the expressive terminology of the red man. 'So long as the rivers run, I shall love you. So long as the grass grows, you are my woman.'

She leaned from the horse a moment, unmindful of Tall Man.

'I am your woman,' she agreed.

The sun was high when they returned, to the acclamation of mountain men and red alike. Big Eagle, propped against a tree, greeted them stoically, but a hint of satisfaction touched his face.

'You do,' he said. 'Good.'

This was not like the rendezvous of past years. But the bitterness, engendered by the news which Irons had brought, was past. A touchy situation had been skirted, and any man with hair tight on his head could feel good. With a right understanding of how they'd been bamboozled, Irons loomed big against the mountains. There were worse things than a break in prices.

The end result might be good. Parks and Higginson were dead, and with no fur bought at any price this season, Parks would find his big house a lonesome place, and serve him right. They'd misdoubted the Mountain, but they knew now who were their friends.

'Turned out pretty good, c'nsiderin',' Shawneen sighed. 'Tough on that Pawnee gal, and on the Black Robe, but they're sure givin' them a right purty funeral. Yeah, this ol' mule could bray, ef'n it wa'n't that he'd rightly be figgered a jackass. Feel kind o' coltish, though, for a fact.'

He was about to say more, but discovered that Irons was no longer listening. He was walking away, Rowena beside him. Misunderstandings had been washed out by the river water. It sure enough looked as if the old Digger had found himself a woman at last. It was a sight to make a man proud, but at the same time to stir the lonesomeness in him.

Off by the tent stood Lexie, proper woman, but looking sort o' lonesome as well. She'd proved out on the trail—good as a squaw. Better in a lot of ways. Likewise, it looked sure enough that they'd be traveling the trail back together, and even though the city lay at the end, he could think of worse things.

No tellin' what *she'd* think of him—he was a gray old badger, for a fact. But there was nothing like finding out. Shawneen looked after Irons again, a tall man with his long-legged stride all but forgotten. Then he headed toward the tent.